"I hope that many will read this heartwarming story and have their faith in humanity restored."

—Rev. Robert M. Hardies,
All Souls Church, Unitarian,
Washington, D.C.

"For most Americans, the word *Hiroshima* summons up an image of the mushroom cloud that resulted from the explosion of the first atomic bomb, but how the everyday people in Hiroshima lived, both before and after the bomb, is often not part of that picture. This book provides a glimpse of that everyday existence through the eyes of a child who was affected by the bomb, certainly, but who found joy in simple pleasures and who was filled with hope, even in the midst of despair. The book thus offers a refreshingly different perspective on one of world history's most pivotal events."

—Gretchen Jones, professor of Japanese literature,
University of Maryland University College

"This is a book that will take your breath away! Shizumi tells the true and heartfelt story of how memories of war define us and change us. . . . The one little cosmos flower brings hope to the world and remains as relevant today as it did in 1945. The book . . . leads into a broader discussion of the ravages of war, the loss of life, and the importance of compassion and forgiveness."

—Portia Davidson, retired workforce-policy advisor to the
commandant of the United States Coast Guard

"A tremendous story that reveals on the personal level the tragic suffering of those at ground zero, how the atomic bomb affected lives, and how the people emerged positive and moving forward. This is a wonderful book with a story that needs to be told."

—Joan Grant, Colorado public-school librarian

"The nuclear devastation and its impact on Hana, who lost her family, is described eloquently. Yet there is a balance in the inspiring and sometimes funny descriptions of the students' school life during the aftermath of the bombing. Just as the paintings the children made of the life they remember and hope for are vivid and colorful, the contrasting passages of Hana's memories before the bomb and her later life create a positive framework for the months of sickness and hunger and horror in the center of the book. The final story of a relationship between the Japanese students and the Americans speaks to the resilience of humans without soft-pedaling the truth of the damage done. Notes at the end of the book will be helpful for using this important book in schools."

—Sally Hamilton, elementary-school teacher, chair of a Japanese-American student exchange program for junior-high students

RUNNING WITH COSMOS FLOWERS

SHIZUMI SHIGETO MANALE and RICHARD MARSHALL

RUNNING
WITH COSMOS
FLOWERS
The CHILDREN of HIROSHIMA

PELICAN PUBLISHING COMPANY
GRETNA 2014

The word "Pelican" and the depiction of a pelican are
trademarks of Pelican Publishing Company, Inc., and are
registered in the U.S. Patent and Trademark Office.

Library of Congress Cataloging-in-Publication Data

Manale, Shizumi Shigeto.
 Running with cosmos flowers : the children of Hiroshima / Shizumi Shigeto
Manale and Richard Marshall.
  pages cm
 Summary: After months of seeking family members with the aunt she was
visiting when Americans dropped an atomic bomb on Hiroshima, Japan, in 1945,
seven-year-old Hanako finally goes back to school and gets on with a life that
leads, eventually, to her visiting Washington, D.C. and the church that provided
them humanitarian aid. Based on first-hand accounts and interviews with
survivors, and illustrated with paintings by Hiroshima children.
 ISBN 978-1-4556-1966-5 (hardcover : alk. paper) — ISBN 978-1-4556-1967-2
(e-book) 1. Hiroshima-shi (Japan)—History—Bombardment, 1945—Juvenile
fiction. [1. Hiroshima-shi (Japan)—History—Bombardment, 1945—Fiction. 2.
Atomic bomb—Fiction. 3. Orphans—Fiction. 4. Survival—Fiction. 5. Japan—
History—1945-1989—Fiction.] I. Marshall, Richard, 1946- II. Title.
 PZ7.M312155Run 2014
 [Fic]—dc23
                              2014017934

*Note: An asterisk marking the first appearance of a certain term indicates that a
definition may be found in the glossary at the back of the book.*

Printed in the United States of America
Published by Pelican Publishing Company, Inc.
1000 Burmaster Street, Gretna, Louisiana 70053

For my mother, Midori Nosohara, and my husband, Andy—S. S. M.

For my father—R. M.

RUNNING WITH COSMOS FLOWERS

CHAPTER ONE

Hanako's Birthday

One morning, I was looking through the *Yomiuri Shimbun* when a headline caught my eye: SCENE OF A DREAM OF HIROSHIMA RESTORED; DRAWINGS WERE 60 YEARS IN WASHINGTON, DC.

It couldn't be. But yes, there it was—my name—and there was my picture, too, just the way I'd drawn it so many years ago. I found myself immediately, an exuberant girl with a white headband, just about to cross the finish line. And then my eye fell on four figures among the crowd of spectators watching me.

In an instant, I'm home again. I am sulking, of course, because my mother is in the country again. But at least I am with my sister, Makiko. Her presence is so vivid that I smell the faint, familiar odor of her hair. It's August fifth, a hot and humid day, but I have my sister with me, and my heart swells with tenderness for her, for she has promised to take me out to the garden and talk to me about its mysteries.

Was that a butterfly that just flew into the window, the foolish thing? She would know its name. The sun's too bright? Better use a parasol.

Is that a leaf fluttering to the ground? Yes, a maple leaf.

I lean against the window, fanning my face with a round *uchiwa* fan. If only autumn would come soon and the war would end. The light from the sun bounces off the glass, making a rainbow. Makiko is outside, calling.

Hanako, come quickly! The lotus buds are quivering; a baby flower is about to blossom. Come now!

I rush out in my bare feet, but it is too late, just as she knew it would be.

Too bad, she says saucily. You missed it. It was like magic. I heard a flower open. Yes, there's a tiny sound, like this—*pon*—and then it opens. And look, a baby lotus flower.

It is beautiful, like a princess in our pond. I am angry for a moment; she should have called me earlier. But who could stay angry at Makiko?

The petals on this lotus flower will close when the sun goes down, she was saying, but tomorrow they will open again. If you wake up early, we can go see them, Hana-chan.

But I won't be home tomorrow, I say. I have to go to Aunt's house again, for my mother was insisting that I go. Will I be able to see the baby lotus flower when I come back?

Of course, my sister says, of course.

I was the only one going to our aunt's house in the country. It didn't seem fair that I wouldn't be able to play with my sister or my friends for another two weeks.

But you'll make new friends at the temple, Makiko said. And there are sure to be lotus flowers in blossom in the pond. It's just going to be for a little while. Mommy will be coming for you soon.

As I looked back, I realized that I could only have had a dim understanding of many things. I was only seven; how could it have been otherwise? I knew, of course, that we, the Japanese, were at war, but I didn't really know what war was or why men fought.

In our garden pond, the lotus-flower princess is shining in the sun. A dragonfly, iridescent red, wings up and settles gently on its brow.

What is it doing on that leaf, Sister Makiko? It looks too busy to be resting. I think it's dancing.

That's the way dragonflies lay their eggs.

This seemed another marvel to me: first the baby lotus flower and now the dancing dragonfly. How many eggs did she lay and how many would hatch? I babbled on. How many would become babies?

And can you really eat dragonflies? The old man next door said he eats grilled frogs *and* dragonflies, but is that true? Even if I get really, really hungry, I would never eat a frog or a dragonfly.

Frogs and dragonflies eat bad insects, she told me. They are God's messengers. We have to take care of them.

Then she bent low to my ear and whispered the word *dragonfly* so that only I could hear, for using English was forbidden at that time. As she did, I saw another, a blue one, light on our stone lantern. The grace of its flight made it, if anything, more beautiful than the iridescent red one. Without thinking, I reached up to touch it, but Makiko stopped me.

You must not do that, Hana-chan. That blue one might be the father of those eggs. There are babies in them.

Then she threw off her serious expression and said gleefully: Let's go swimming. We can find more dragonflies there and practice swimming too.

I'll race you, and off we flew in our bare feet all the way to the water's edge.

It was easy enough: the Motoyasu River was just behind our house. All we had to do was climb over the backyard fence and there it was, the cool, clear river. Although it was still morning, the sun was already hot, and there were many children in the water or on the embankments.

Makiko, my teacher in so many things, had decided it was time I learned to swim. She was wonderfully patient with me and stayed at her task despite the pleas of her friends to join them. Her smooth face, the disappearing dimples in her cheeks, and her deep, dark eyes filled the sky above me as I kicked and splashed. My sister. But there was something else about her today, something that made her start at times and look up sharply toward the sky, as though she were looking for something she could not share with me.

A boy about my sister's age came swimming up to us. His eyesight must have been pretty bad because even in the water he wore glasses. I thought that was funny.

Hey, Makiko, he said to her in that teasing way boys have.

How'd you like to take my turn this afternoon? I'll stay here and swim, and you can stand guard and see if any enemy planes fly over.

But my sister paid him no attention. She nudged me and pointed to the river bottom. Today's our lucky day, she said. For the bed was lined with tiny round *shijimi* clams, which we put in our morning miso soup whenever we could find them. I reached down and brought up a handful and showed them to Makiko. And she smiled at me.

Grandma appeared, looking stern and out of sorts. The time was slipping by and she hurried us back to the house. With my sister's help, I would pack a few things to take to my aunt's. I hated these so-called evacuations, but there was nothing to be done about it. I had to go and they had to stay.

Birthdays were not so important then as now. We normally only celebrated when someone turned three or five or seven, for those were important numbers. I was hoping, of course, that someone would remember it was my seventh birthday. But so far no one had.

To my surprise, when we got back to the house my grandmother's expression suddenly brightened. She had remembered, after all. Using millet and the last of the rice flour from the bin, she'd made sweet *kibi dango*, brown-rice dumplings, and with a warm smile, she put some in my hand and some others in my pack.

Grandma, what will we do now that you have used all the rice flour? my sister asked.

We'll be fine, she answered softly. We still have some dumplings, and we'll get some more rice when your mother comes back tonight. You don't need to worry, she said, putting her hand on my head with a warmth and affection that made me feel safe and comforted.

It was time to go. Makiko waved goodbye to me, and the dimples in her cheeks that only came out when she smiled reappeared.

Goodbye, Hana-chan. I'll take good care of those dragonfly eggs.

Be sure to tell me how many babies there are, I called back. I'll bring home lots of rice.

Then, I hurried off to the station with my grandmother to catch the coal bus to my aunt's house.

Good-Luck *Omamori**

We had to change buses twice, so by the time we arrived at my aunt's farm it was late afternoon. All the way I counted the minutes until I could see my mother. She was a teacher and was assigned to go with her pupils to stay at a temple in the country, sometimes for weeks at a time. It hardly seemed fair that they got to spend so much time with her and I did not.

People talked about the war all the time, and particularly the bombings, but they were in Tokyo and other places far away. But never in Hiroshima, where I live. What I hated most about the war was this: that my mother was gone so often. My father I hardly knew.

Now I had finally seen her again and clung to her and felt the love and reassurance I so badly wanted. But she was preparing to go again, returning to the city that evening with her charges. I wanted more than anything to go with her. But no—evacuation it had to be.

I watched her strap my baby brother, Tadashi, on her back and fill a small wheelbarrow with sacks of good white rice. She went about it carefully, as she went about most things, pacing slowly around the thing, seeing the way the weight was balanced. I wanted her to hold me and take me with her. I was crying, begging, in front of the other children. But already, it was late.

Only when they were ready to leave did my mother look at me.

Here, my little Hana-chan, I have something for you. I am sorry that I could not do more, but this is a birthday charm, a silver *omamori* from the Senkyo Temple.

May it protect you against all harm. I have prayed for your health and good luck, my dearest and most precious child. Happy birthday to you. *Omedetou!*

She had not forgotten. Despite all the hardships of the war, she had remembered my birthday. Even so, when she went to leave,

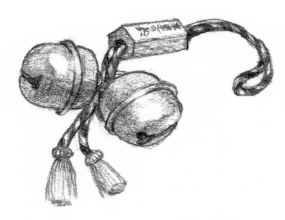

Omamori. (Drawing by Yoshiko Jaeggi, courtesy of Shizumi Shigeto Manale)

I could not help but cry again and I pleaded with her to let me go with her.

After a moment, Grandma came and took me gently by the hand. Don't worry, she said. We will come back and bring you home soon.

But I want to go home! I cried. I want to go home.

My mother only turned and wiped away my tears. You have to stay, my little girl, she said, just a little while this time. I'll be back and then we can go home together. Yes, I promise. So please don't cry or you will make me cry too, and I don't want to do that in front of my students.

And she took my hand and opened my fingers and shook the tiny silver bells. They made a wonderful clear sound, rich in color and overtones. Then she put them in my hand again and gently closed it shut.

Now it was time for my aunt to speak. Hurry, Sister. These children must be going. She turned away, but I was listening and overheard her say something about enemy planes, Americans, coming from across the mountains, and in an instant my mother had lined up her pupils and they were gone.

My aunt and I watched, and we waved until their shadows disappeared down the curving mountain road.

A Gift from Kyushu

That evening my uncle came home unexpectedly from the Miike coalmines on Kyushu Island. He looked gaunt and grey but very pleased to see my aunt. She was pregnant, and he had been very worried about her.

I felt lonely staying in that large house but a little more secure with my uncle there. He had brought me a special present, too: a *zabon mikan*, a big round orange from Kyushu.

The *zabon mikan* had a beautiful smell. I was feeling ashamed of myself for having acted so childishly with my mother in front of the other children, so to make up for it, I decided not to touch the orange but wait until I could share it with Makiko, who had been so nice to me earlier that day.

Mushroom Cloud

I had often heard their urgent voices when there were air raids, my mother and the others. Quick, Hanako. Hurry, child. Turn off the lights. Move. Inside the shelter. Hurry—you must hurry, please. And they were saying America is the cause of all this, and the Emperor won't let it happen, and, finally, there's not much rice left. Air raids, airplanes, B-29 bombers, and the terrible destruction. *Tenno-heika, Banzai!* Long live the Emperor!

Every day we used to gather at the temple grounds to practice fighting in case our evil enemy ever dared attack. Under the guidance of a few old men, we learned how to thrust and parry with pointed bamboo poles. We would show the *beigun,** the American enemies; we'd fight to the death to protect our Emperor.

Secretly, of course, I thought it was a lot of fun. I loved to run alongside the other children, yelling and screaming with imagined fury, my bamboo pole outstretched as I charged the dummy. It had an ugly demon's face and was filled with straw, and they'd hung it from a pine tree in the gardens. We pummeled it with blows and went home tired but satisfied.

It was just before eight the next morning when my uncle turned on the radio. I was drinking my miso soup, half-asleep, when I heard a news bulletin. There was an urgency to the man's voice, and I remember my uncle jumping to his feet.

A B-29 has been seen over Fukuyama, he screamed. It's over Onomichi now and heading this way!

We have to take shelter immediately! Run, hurry, hurry, he shouted, but I just stood there in confusion while he raced out to get my aunt.

She's doing the wash in the back of the farmhouse and does not hear him shout. It takes her a minute to drop the clothes and dry her hands, and my uncle is pulling at her to get her moving. Together they race for the door, and then the house begins to shake.

An earthquake! my aunt yells, grabbing my uncle by the arm. It's an earthquake.

The quake is very strong now and making an awful rumbling sound. I stagger and fall, and the wooden case that holds their shoes tumbles on top of me. I hear a crash from the inner room; the altar has fallen over. Out of the corner of my eye, I see their little gold Buddha go flying through the air and out of sight. Our ancestors are fleeing; how could that be?

For a long time all is dust, with that terrible *churring* noise and the terrifying quaking. I scream for my mother and squeeze my good-luck *omamori* with all my might. Finally, my aunt pulls the case off me, cradling the baby in her belly with one hand, and together we all creep beneath the eating table.

Her face is cut in a few places and she keeps saying, an earthquake, an earthquake, a monstrous earthquake, over and over as she wipes the blood from her face with a cotton towel.

My uncle is bleeding, too, and his white shirt is torn. But no one is badly hurt, and at some point he goes out and brings us water and a blanket and squeezes back under the table with us.

How long we were there, wrapped together in that blanket, I cannot tell. It could have been five minutes, or it could have been an hour. At last, the shaking subsided; slowly we unfolded ourselves and came out.

The house was a shambles. I could scarcely comprehend what had happened. The Emperor's picture had fallen and the frame was cracked. There was furniture scattered everywhere and most of my aunt's plates were lying broken on the floor. Outside, several tiles had blown off the roof, but it was a solid house and the rest of it was still intact.

My uncle gathered us in his arms and then went to look for his radio. Somehow, he found it and managed to get it working. I watched as he held it to his ear. Suddenly he turned and cried in an anguished voice to my aunt, A huge bomb—they dropped a huge bomb on Hiroshima. The whole city is on fire.

Bitter curses rained from his tongue as he rushed us toward the village shelter. What have they done to us, these American bastards? he cried. Is there no end to their cruelty?

Please, please, we have to hurry. The B-29s could be here at any time.

As we were running, I saw a man, a neighbor of my aunt and uncle's, pointing toward the mountain beyond which lay the city of Hiroshima. Racing high above it, filling the sky with fury, was a huge cloud of horrid swirling air. The sight of this enormous black cloud, so sinister, so much more menacing than anything I could conceive, struck such fear in me that I, that I . . . have never spoken of it until this moment.

Would to God that I never saw a mushroom cloud. I pray that no one else will ever have to see one.

Inside the shelter it was as dark as night. Carved out of the rocks on the side of a hill behind the town hall, it was more like a cave than the shelter we had at home. There were about twenty of us, pressed together like a family of moles, scared and whispering, Was it an earthquake?

No, probably some bombs. In the city.

Bombs? In the city? How could that be? The city is so far away. It must have been an earthquake.

Such terrible luck, our neighbors muttered, such terrible luck. The war, the *gaijin,** and their cowardly bombs—and now the city is on fire. What if they bomb us too?

But why would they want to? What have we done?

After a while, the men gathered up their courage and went outside. There were no planes in the air, at least for now, and so they brought us out into a world that would never be the same. We shook off the dirt and looked up at the thick red haze as if seeking a message from the gods. But the gods had flown away.

Sunset

A sunset the color of dried blood lay over the basin where the city of Hiroshima once stood. The old women of my aunt's village, the ones whose work was never done, stood by stunned, casting vague, uncomprehending glances toward the sky. What was this haze? No one spoke; no one knew.

Details of the destruction came in bits and pieces over my uncle's radio, and late that afternoon he and some other men from the village loaded their carts with rice and barley and left for the city. Cleaning up the village of Hon-chii would be the women's work.

The first of the wounded began streaming in that night. They came like ghostlike *yurai** in the eerie reddish twilight, their faces chalky and the skin hanging from their arms in strips, stalking the silent streets like skeletons in search of their own spirits.

A few of the stronger ones were pulling carts, some of which had dead bodies on them. Many survivors were burnt, terribly, painfully so, and their clothes were singed and stuck to their skin where the blood had dried and caked. Worst of all, to my young senses, was the smell: pungent, putrid, awful. It was a smell I would have to learn to live with.

White Silk *Juban**

By the next morning the village was crowded with these *yurai* ghosts, pale, charred figures, their lives and clothes in tatters. Their suffering transcended the small places where they lay and filled Hon-chii with their agony and cries for justice and relief.

My uncle was the village headman. He was the fifth generation of his family to hold the position, and his house was the largest in the village. So perhaps it was natural that he and my aunt opened it as a shelter. I watched in silence as she and the other women spread mats on the earth floor and, when there was no more space, out under the shade trees in the garden.

We need iodine, more Mercurochrome. Where are the bandages? Hurry—bring that hot water here. Help! Can't anybody help? I heard them crying, each voice more urgent than the other. But another voice was crying in me, much louder and more urgent than any of these strangers: my mother. Where was she? Where was she when I longed for her so much?

At length, my aunt came up to me and hugged me in her arms. Soon, too soon, she pulled back and resumed her firm expression.

Don't ask too many questions, Hana-chan. Not now. We just don't know the answers. In the meantime, we have work to do. Please, help me make these bandages.

But I pestered her with questions about my mother, our house, my sister, Makiko. Was everybody safe?

They are safe, she said. They must have gone to an evacuation center. They would be okay. They must be.

Together we tore up sheets. I went with her among the burnt and battered figures lying on the mats. Some of them were with their families, anxious huddles of people grieving their missing members.

One man in particular I remember: his face was covered with an old green cloth, and it had stuck where his eye should have been. My aunt had to change the cloth, and she stooped low to him and removed that horrid thing, blackened with the blood that had seeped through, and replaced it with her own white sheeting, and I grew woozy and the room spun around and I stumbled out of the room and fell into a kind of sleep.

When I came to, I was in the closet where she stored the futons and she was cradling me in her arms. I heard her crying softly. They had been looking for me everywhere, everywhere. After I could stand, she took my hand and we went back to making bandages.

By evening, there was no more space in the house or garden. Smell is a sharp sense, but it loses its sharpness quickly. Gradually, I forgot about the foul odor all around me and began to venture out among the strangers who lay suffering on the mats. Out in the back I found a girl under a mosquito net who looked familiar: my sister's friend Yuko.

Yuko-chan? Is that you?

Hana-chan. What are you doing here? Are you okay? Where is Makiko-chan?

We didn't know. No one knew. I asked her where my mother was. Was she safe; where could she be? She had no news and that frightened me terribly. But there was no time for that now. I looked at Yuko-chan. Her pants and blouse were smeared with grime, but, to my great relief, she had not been hurt.

Who is that? I asked in respectful words and voice about the person next to her.

It's my mother, she said.

I couldn't say anything for a while. She must have been suffering terribly. I brought them water; thank God we still had that.

Yuko-chan asked: Do you have anything for her—bandages, clothes, or cotton rags, anything—that I can bandage her with?

We did not have a sheet or shirt or piece of cloth that had not been cut up already. I knew that, but I went to my aunt and told her about Makiko's friend Yuko and her mother.

She had worked herself beyond the limits of endurance, my aunt, and was just sitting, cross-legged, on her bed mat, unable to sleep or stay awake.

Yuko-chan's mother is about to die, she said quietly, raising her eyes to mine. There is nothing we can do. With that she lay on the mat and curled herself up on one side as if to sleep. Instinctively, she reached out to draw me to her side. But then, after we had lain there briefly, she rose and drew a long, slow breath and went to the other room, stepping with great care over the smoldering ruins of people's lives, and back she came with a white silk *juban* wrapped in a fine rice paper.

We stepped our way back through the room and out into the

garden. It was easier now: I was learning not to see some things. I helped Yuko wash and powder her mother's face, filling the air with a fragrance of unexpected elegance. Then she and my aunt slipped the *juban* around her, taking great pains not to hurt her and adjusting it until it fit her well, and that was the way she died.

Senkyo Temple

Day after day they came, the burnt, the broken, and the bitter. My uncle came back from the city on his bicycle, pulling and walking a two-wheeled cart up to Hon-chii with five people on it. My mother, I thought, it must be my mother and the rest of them, Makiko, the baby, my grandmother, even my father would be there, hurt, perhaps, but not too badly. Surely, if anyone had found them, it would be my uncle. I rushed out to see.

But no. Uncle took a short rest, and then he and my aunt loaded rice sacks in his cart and he set off again for Hiroshima.

They'd opened the wide hall of the Senkyo Temple to the displaced, and we went there to see if my mother or any of my family might be there, or if anyone might know anything about them. The hall, where just days ago we had sat listening to the monks, was now filled with the torments of the burn victims and those who were trying to help them.

I noticed a boy about the same age as my sister, his eyes covered with cloth bandages red with recent blood.

Poor boy, my aunt said, the force of the explosion drove his glasses into his eyes. Can you give him water, Hanako?

I did and he clutched my hand. It was the boy from the Motoyasu, the one who wanted Makiko to take his sentry duty. What will happen to him? I asked. Will he lose his sight?

But my aunt said nothing, just did what she could for him, then took me by the hand and we went among the suffering strangers, looking, looking.

They tried to keep things from me, but I overheard my aunt, outside in the dark one night, talking to the neighbors about what my uncle had seen.

In the center, there's nothing left of the city, nothing standing: not a house, not a tree, not a single living thing. There are fires everywhere. They set it all on fire, she said bitterly. They destroyed our Hiroshima.

I don't know; I don't know, she whispered sadly as they crowded around her with questions of this relative or that. There may be survivors, she said. They think so, but nobody knows. It's impossible to find out anything, impossible to know. What I do know is this. My husband says that afterward, after their awful earthquake bomb, people ran out of their homes and down to the water, everybody who could walk or crawl, anything, just to get to the water. But nobody could help them. It was horrible, horrible, thousands and tens of thousands of corpses in the river. The smell had been unbearable. That was all she could tell them.

They began to weep and moan, and I know she wept with them, but after a while I heard her speak again.

It's up to us women, she said. We are the survivors; we'll have to work even harder now.

I had still heard nothing about my family. I missed my mother so intensely that she stayed in my thoughts day and night, and I often found myself dreaming of her and feeling her hold me closely in her arms.

News of the bombing kept trickling in, especially in the rare moments when my uncle was at home, but there was nothing about what mattered most. They tried to shield me from it, but somehow I'd heard enough to harbor many fears. At least my mother was safe, even if we can't find her, I told myself. Aunt had said so. Besides, I always had my good luck *omamori*, and I rang its silver chimes for my mother all day and night.

We spent the days in work and worry. Gradually, the victims left my aunt's house; either they died or found a hospital or clinic that could take them. On the radio we'd heard of another bombing, this time in Nagasaki, and a report saying that parts of Hiroshima were still burning. Only people involved in emergency relief, like my uncle, could get through. That was a harrowing time for my aunt and me. We both desperately wanted to get to

Hiroshima and find out what happened to my mother and my aunt's younger son, Hideki. He had been working in the city when the bomb struck and had not been seen since then, and she was frantic to find him.

As soon as the fires were out, she'd gone down to the city. This time for sure, I told myself, she'd find my mother, and I pictured how they'd be coming, walking together, tired after the long journey, perhaps, but she'd be alive and well and here with me.

Aunt came home alone. I couldn't find anyone, she said wearily, not my son, or your mother, or your sister, or anybody. There's so much . . . destruction, it's awful, awful. It's impossible to get around. No one has any information. They could be anywhere.

They're probably at an emergency center, one of her neighbors volunteered, or at a hospital getting treatment.

Yes, they probably are, my aunt agreed. They probably are. I'm going back tomorrow to keep looking.

Let's go back now, I insisted. I want to go home. I want to see my mother. I want to see my sister and my dragonfly babies. My aunt looked up and a tender flicker of a smile crossed her face.

I wish I could take you to see the baby dragonflies, my little one, she said. But that's no place for a young child. Not yet. It's just not safe.

Otoh-chan (Father) and Okaa-chan (Mother)

Two. Two? What are you? I am one and I am two. Two eyes? Two ears, too. Are there any more twos for you? Yes, my mother's warm, sweet hands make two.

I am in the courtyard of an emergency center they'd set up in a temple a few kilometers from Hon-chii. There are soldiers everywhere and lines and lines of nervous, angry people. But I'm watching a little girl sing the numbers song. I know that song, every child does, so we sing it together. Two, two, what are you? One and two, two eyes, two ears too.

Turning around, I see my shadow lengthening in the afternoon sun. It's fun to pretend I'm a sumo wrestler and step like a giant over the little girl's shadow, then watch her try to do the same to mine. I move and she steps on my shadow and I cry out as if in great pain. She laughs and I find myself laughing too, but then I catch myself and stop.

After a while my aunt comes out of the temple, looking anxiously for me. She grabs my hand and off we set across the battered bridge, walking swiftly. It's only then that I realize that she thought she'd lost me in the crowd.

Hana-chan, I think they've found your father, she says in a low voice. They say he's in the emergency clinic. Tomorrow we'll go and see him.

We could not go that night. No one dared to stay outside after darkness fell. The *yurai* ghosts came walking then. I'd seen them once and lay in terror of them every night.

I was glad, of course, that they had found my father. But why couldn't it have been my mother or my grandmother? And where was Sister Makiko? But my aunt didn't know. I only know that your father is alive, she said. Tomorrow we will go and find him.

The next morning we got up early and hopped aboard the little cart so my uncle could pull us behind his bicycle. On the way she talked to me of my father, of the things he had done in the army, where he had gone, the campaign medals he had won, the man he had been before the war.

The road had many twists and turns as it dropped down toward Hiroshima and at one we caught a clear view of what lay below. Even now, I can see it, the grey-black, smoldering cinders of the ruined city, the devastated streets and buildings stretching out for miles, the charcoal-colored stumps and trees. No child should have to see these things.

We drove on in heavy silence, out of the green country, trailing behind my uncle's bike. We could smell the city before we got to it. My aunt had brought cotton, which we placed up our noses, and we covered our faces with *tenugui* cotton towels, and still it didn't help that much.

Hiroshima, as seen from Honkawa School, 1945. (Courtesy of Honkawa Elementary School, Hiroshima)

At first there are only a few indications, as if warnings, of what lies ahead of us: some shattered windows, a broken roof, smoke rising in the distance. We drive on; the road is rough now and my uncle has to stop at times, and then it gets so bad we have to get out and walk, over the rubble . . . the heaps of rubble, the homes and shops and offices that used to be so full of life. . . .

At one point a policeman stops us and asks us where we're going. He's not much older than Makiko and missing the lower part of his arm. My uncle salutes when he sees that and tells him the name of the emergency center we're looking for. We walk on. Most of the bridges are broken, half-toppled into the river, but finally we find one that we can get across.

They'd set up the center in a post office. It had been a solid building and most of it was still intact. Inside, they'd laid down rows of wooden boards for beds. Pain was everywhere you looked, on the planks and under the bloody sheets, and in faces of the people who stood by helplessly, looking, looking. I knew it now, that looking, and that brought back the fear. I shut my eyes and tried to shut it out.

We finally found my father, lying on a board with two other men in a crowded room somewhere on the second floor. At first I did not recognize him. I almost wish I never had.

Hana-chan, my aunt said. It's Otoh-chan, your father. Go to him. She motioned to me, but I held back. I was scared to approach him, for fear, I am ashamed to say, that I'd be compelled to hug him.

He seemed to understand that and smiled at me. I went and stood by his bed and bowed. His face was swollen and there were tears in his eyes. Hana-chan, my baby girl, he said with great effort. You're alive. You're alive and you're safe. So good. So good.

There was little left of him beneath the blanket, I could see that much. It took a long time to understand. I had not been hurt and so many others had. Now, as I see my father's face again, it is in this dark-blue room, across a sea of troubled, purple faces.

But I try not to think of them, only of my duty. I draw my lips tight and smile. I hold his good hand; the other one is burnt all the way through to the bone and dreadful to look at.

These are not the hands of my father, I think. They belong to some other man. I cannot look directly at him—my own father.

Otoh-chan, it must be so very painful, I finally say. I am so sorry, so sorry, and I turn to my aunt and bury my head in her bosom and cry.

But what is this? He knows where my mother and baby brother are? Or so I hear him tell my aunt. He is weeping now and labors to speak, like an old man, weary of the world.

Okaa-chan and Tadashi are in . . . the other room, he says through the pain.

My heart bursts with happiness. My mother is alive. My wish has come true. I want so much to believe it that I ask him to say it again, where she is and who is with her, but my aunt just puts her finger on my lips.

No more questions, child. Your father needs to rest. You stay here quietly with him. I'll be back as soon as I can.

I harbor such a longing for my mother that, even with my father now, I cannot hide my feelings, and I chatter on about all the things that we will do when I see her again. He smiles briefly, and I pull out my silver *omamori* and ring its silver bells for him. After so many days and nights, I am going to see my Okaa-chan.

It seems as though my aunt is gone for hours. Where is my mother? I have to see her. Where is her bed mat? Without knowing it, I start walking around the room, disturbing people, asking if they know where my mother is. Okaa-chan, Okaa-chan, where are you? All the time I am praying that she's not burnt, maybe just a little if it has to be, but not like my father.

I cannot find her in the crowded room. I return to my father; his eyes are closed; only his lips are twitching slightly. He awakes when I take his hand, and he asks for water. I help him drink, the way my aunt has taught me: one hand on top, one hand on the bottom.

Thank you, my little Hana-chan, he says, so softly that I have to bend low to hear, and the odor—sweat and dirt and rotting flesh—is almost overwhelming. At last my aunt appears. I run to her. Surely, my mother is right behind her. But her eyes show only sorrow. And then I see: a little wooden box, wrapped in white cotton cloth.

Where is Okaa-chan? I demand. Take me to her now.

But my aunt just shakes her head. Can't you understand? she finally asks. Your mother and Tadashi-chan are here, in this box.

But how could she be in such a tiny box? I cry in desperate confusion.

Poor Hana-chan, she says sadly. Okaa-chan and Tadashi-chan have passed away. They are watching you from heaven now. We must pray for them. Their spirits are counting on you. You must be good and show them what a good daughter you can be.

I hardly hear half of what she's saying. I cannot understand. Okaa-chan cannot be in that tiny box, I scream. She can't be in there. She promised to come to see me.

My poor aunt said nothing. She went to hug me but I pushed her away. Everyone near us had been listening to our conversation and many of the women were weeping with us, and for themselves as well.

Nobody can come back from death, my aunt told me as we made our way through the edges of the devastated city. We can't change that. And we can't change this, this horror that's all around us.

All the way to Hon-chii she let me cry. We'd never found her little gold Buddha and when we got to my aunt's home, she put my mother and baby brother on the altar, where the Buddha used to be. Many times I came to look at them, resting in their tiny box. It must be very painful, I thought, to be squeezed into such a space. Yet they were together, and I was alone.

The next night my uncle came home with another little wooden box, this one with my father in it. He said nothing but placed it quietly on the altar, next to my mother and Tadashi. Later that night I saw him reach in his pocket and put something on the table. I only saw it for a second, but I knew what it was instantly: my mother's glasses.

One lens was missing and the other was cracked, and the frames, which had partly melted, were stretched in odd, extruded shapes.

My aunt glared at him, then reached out and took them and put them in her pocket. What are you doing? she hissed. Then she bowed her head for a long minute and went and put them on the altar, too.

How easy it was to see my mother in my imagination then. Her smiling face was my constant companion. I'd taken to wearing the good-luck bells around my neck, tied to a ribbon that she'd given me and to which, it seemed to my disordered mind, a trace of her scent still clung. Sometimes I would talk to my sister too, about a flower that was blooming or a grasshopper that I'd caught, and how an evil bomb had fallen from the sky and sent Okaa-chan and Tadashi to heaven. And now my father had gone to join them.

Uncle passed his hand through his hair and pulled a few

strands free. He shook them off and turned away. Try as he might, he'd been unable to find information about their son or my grandmother, but he had heard from someone who thought they'd seen my sister walking on the Aioi Bridge.

As soon as my aunt heard this, she began to pack her things. Where are you going? my uncle asked.

No more coming and going, she said. Hanako and I are going to Hiroshima. I am going to look for my son. And Makiko.

How can you find someone who isn't there? he hurled back at her.

You can't find them, but maybe I can, she shot back. Let me try at least.

But where will you stay?

There's a shelter just outside of town. I heard it on the radio.

Well, you should leave Hana-chan here, he said. That's no place for her; leave her with the neighbors.

What, and let her wander the streets? My aunt would not hear of it. For the village was not the same as before. There were strangers everywhere, odd, sick, and injured people, sad, deformed, and damaged people, burnt, bewildered, and pain-wracked.

Among them were many children, alone and hungry, desperately looking for their parents and their families. But no one could help them, or would, or so it seemed, for everyone had his own catastrophe, and after a while people stopped seeing them, as if they had become invisible, or worse, an irritant, like mosquitoes.

That night I prayed that we would find my sister. I imagined how it would be when I saw her again. I practiced many clever things to say. I had heard my uncle's warning, though, and wondered how we'd find her. For how can you find someone who is not there—unless you have a lucky *omamori?*

The Emperor's Voice

She woke me in the early hours. We ate our rice without a word and left before the sun came up. There was a coal bus running from the village again that took you to the outskirts of the city. After that you had to walk. There were many people like us on the road, carrying packs and pulling carts.

What was my sister wearing when they saw her? I asked my aunt. Did she have her blue kerchief on? And why didn't this bus take us all the way to the river like the old one used to?

I pestered her and pestered her until finally she turned on me and said: You are old enough to understand what has happened, Hana-chan. What you see is real. I wish I could change it for you, pretend that all this is just a terrible dream. But it isn't. All this, everything you see, everything you know and learned is gone. Everything has changed.

The August sun beat down on us as we walked along the broken road toward the river and the center of the town. Beads of sweat collected on our foreheads and under our straw hats. My aunt was walking quickly now, covering her face with a *tenugui* towel tucked at one end under her hat. She was heavy with the child and breathing hard.

We sat for a bit on the side of the road. Then she rose and we started down a path that twisted between the piles of rubble. Everywhere was the same charred mess. We saw a man lying on the roadside. My aunt approached, to see if he was alive or not, then bowed briefly, put her hands together, prayed, and started walking once again. He's already passed away, she said with a sigh. I'm sorry for him.

I am sorry for him too, I replied. But I was getting used to saying that and meaning it less and less. It took a long time to understand. Of course, I'd seen a lot of people suffering from their wounds and dying of them, and I'd lost my fear of that—no, not my fear, so much as the ability to be shocked by it. The pain I stored in a spot so far away it would take me sixty years to find it.

As we went on, we saw two figures lying in the shadow of a solitary wall. One was small, like a child, with a heavily bandaged leg, and the other a woman of uncertain age. My aunt hesitated to approach, guessing they too might be dead. But she composed herself and went up to them. The child had passed to heaven—I could have told her that—but the woman was still alive and my aunt lifted her head gently and cradled it in her arms, calling to me to bring the water pitcher. I felt glad that the woman was still alive and rushed to help her. My aunt tried to give her water, but either she was too weak to take it or too far gone.

I don' wanna die, she kept repeating deliriously. I don' wanna die.

We ran back to the main road to look for help. We had done what we could. Couldn't somebody help her, take her to an emergency center? We asked and asked, but nobody paid us any notion. Nobody had the time. That too had been destroyed.

But we were no different from the others, and regretfully we turned and started walking again under the glaring sun, and watching the sky. There were enemy planes in the sky every day now and we were all terrified that they might drop another bomb at any moment.

On the way, a man pulling a two-wheeled cart behind his bicycle stopped and asked if we'd like a ride. It must be hard for you, he said to my aunt, bowing vaguely toward her belly. Hop on board.

With that, he got off and helped her up onto a wooden crate. He sat me on a stack of sandbags. For some reason I remember this experience with great clarity—perhaps because it was fun to sit in the back of a cart, swaying on a stack of sandbags and looking down on everyone we passed. Without thinking about it, I started singing the counting song again, numbering the trees and talking to my sister. But my aunt and the man who was pulling us remained silent all the way.

They were beginning to haul away the debris from a few main streets, but most roads were impassable, save for the narrow paths that cut across the piles of pulverized concrete. Not far from the central plaza, near the Military Police Headquarters, our new friend stopped pedaling, and we scurried out of the cart. People were coming into the plaza in great numbers, bitter, ragged, determined people, and there were soldiers everywhere, standing at attention and raising their arms in brisk salute.

Somebody was saying something over the loudspeakers. My aunt and the man jumped to attention, straight as soldiers, and I followed suit, not knowing why.

Tenno-heika, Banzai! Long live the Emperor! a voice cried out. I turned and saw a man holding his military cap high above his head, as if in triumph.

But as the sound of the Emperor's voice came over the loudspeakers, everyone bowed. Many were weeping. I couldn't understand. I looked around; there were men and women of all ages, standing or kneeling on the ground, sobbing bitterly. Others covered their faces. One old man collapsed on the ground as if stricken with a heart attack, his body shaking.

Why are they crying? I asked my aunt. What has happened now? But she just shook her head and turned away. The man refused to answer too, just stared emptily into space, his head to one side. Then he too went down on his knees, his head sunk on the sooty ground.

Then one by one the soldiers who had been standing so smartly at attention dropped to the ground, sitting with their legs beneath them, *seiza*-style.*

These brave men wept. The shame of it, they said. Japan had lost the war. How could it be? We were winning. That's what they told us. We were winning, and now, surrender, defeat. After all these years of sacrifice, what would become of us?

This moment of surrender was the first time we'd ever heard the Emperor's voice. Until then, he'd been a god. But now the gods had flown away. I knew. I'd seen them fly.

CHAPTER TWO

Home

We thanked our friend and started off again, charting our direction by the Hiroshima Prefectural Hall.* The walls had all come down, but somehow the dome in the center of it was still standing, the tallest structure in the impact zone.

We turn here, my aunt says. It's not far to the house. A dead horse, charred crisp and smelling so bad I have to hold my nose, is lying in our path. We have no choice but to step over it. The carcass is covered with flies. I want to vomit.

I never imagined a horse could be so big, but my aunt says that sometimes they swell up like that if no one buries them. For some reason this bothers me and I ask her why no one has taken care of the poor thing. Doesn't it have a spirit too?

But she just says, Please, child, we've got more important things to do than worry about dead horses.

The smell of dust and mildew and pulverized concrete mixed with rotting bodies hangs over everything, the sum total of an entire city carbonized. Everywhere and everything is black, the battered, tattered, bewildered strangers, the rubble-pile homes, the scorched tree trunks. Everything is singed. Only the sky is clean, and yet it is from this sky that a bomb has fallen that could leave the land and our lives like this.

Small puddles of people drift past us as we head down Honkawa Avenue, looking, looking. While my aunt worries about her son, my mind is full of Makiko. I see her in every distant figure, only

to suffer disappointment each and every time. No one has seen or
heard of her. Few have time to talk.

Not far from us is the steel factory where my cousin Hideki
used to work. It is still smoldering, and there are soldiers there
who order us away.

No, they say, we have no information. Now go. Go.

We walk a few minutes and then my aunt stops and takes her
backpack off and sits down on the ground. That is the last time I
ever see her cry.

After a while, there is nothing for us to do but walk. As we pass
them, my aunt keeps saying I'm sorry to the people we encounter.
I am sorry, so very sorry. But after a while she can't see the point
anymore and falls silent, as if, perhaps, she's drunk her cup of
sorrow but cannot find the bottom.

I feel scared of the people we are seeing now, the way they pass
in angry silence. I try to close my eyes to them and the horror that
stretches for block after block in every direction. I am focused on
my house. The closer we get to it, the closer we get to the truth.

How my aunt finds our street is a mystery. There are no more
roads, no landmarks; the few trees standing are standing charcoal.
At last we arrive. My heart is pounding, for in it a dream still lives,
that somehow my mother will be here, waiting for me. And yet I
know it cannot be. For I had seen the truth, held it in a tiny box,
and breathed it in every breath of foul air since yesterday. I know
and yet I guess I don't know.

My house is gone; it's disappeared. I scream and scream.
Nothing remains. The rooms I'd lived in all my life are gone.
Everything is ash and trash. But memory is an uncanny thing.
Even today, I can place those rooms exactly: here is the entrance,
there the living room. This is the bedroom I shared with Sister
Makiko, and there's where my mother and baby Tadashi-chan
slept.

We begin a careful circle around the heap that used to be my
home. It takes me a long time to understand. But it's just a matter
of simple physics. At a certain temperature everything burns:
timber, cloth, and human beings.

Ah, they've been here already, my aunt says, the thieves. They've come and stolen the pipes. Good, solid pipes they were, too; I helped to lay them myself.

I watch as she piles blocks of jagged concrete at the edges of where she thinks our land must lie. It's hard work, and she's breathing hard, and after a while I have to stop thinking of myself and join her, for there's the baby coming. I follow her out to where our garden used to be. We know it because of the pond. There's no water left, but the rocks on the bottom are still there, cracked and scarred with soot, and the skeletons of two carp, my grandfather's favorites, like silhouettes, are baked into the surface of the stone.

Our stone lantern is here, cracked but still standing guard, and now there's a dark red stain on one side, like a shadow of a tree. At least they hadn't taken that. But my aunt just scoffs. Hardly worth stealing, is how she puts it. And as for the lotus blossoms, only their memory is left. That too is a hard lesson for me.

My aunt is pushing herself to exhaustion and I finally have to tell her to stop. A strange red sun is setting in a strange orange sky. It's hell, she finally says, hell on earth. What have we done? This misery, devastation, the death of every living thing: what have we done? What have we done to deserve it?

I'm sure she would have cried if she could have. For a long time we just sat there, stunned, trying not to see. But it was getting dark and my aunt righted herself. The *yurai* ghosts would be coming out and we didn't want to see them.

But it was not the *yurai* that my aunt was worried about. It was the half-mad people we had to go amongst, and we had a long hour's walk ahead of us before we would get to the Gokoku Shinto Shrine, where my uncle was to meet us.

We are going to spend the night in a shelter there, she told me. We may have to stay there a while. Uncle would join us, though; that was the most important thing.

But Uncle didn't come to the Gokoku Shrine. We waited and waited; we waited until we couldn't wait a minute longer. He couldn't have missed this place, she said. Even now, like this, how could he have missed it? Something must have happened.

By then they had no room for us at the shrine. We tried three other shelters, but every one was full. What if we had to sleep outside? The thought drove us on through the frightful Hiroshima night.

There were strange flashes in the darkness, like silver fireflies. What could they mean? I asked my aunt.

Spirits, she replied. Those are the spirits of the dead rising up to heaven.

My poor aunt, I must have been a burden to her; a seven-year-old can only be a burden. At some point—I only half-remember a dark street and the terror we felt all around us—a truck came up and a volunteer came out and talked to my aunt, and then she bowed to him and said, I appreciate your kindness. I remember that for some reason: I appreciate your kindness.

They hauled us up in the back of the truck and drove us to a shelter. This one had some space, they said, but it was so crowded there was hardly a place to stand. It was hot and hard to breathe and it reeked of a thousand unwashed bodies. Here and there the floor was broken up, and worse, the mosquitoes and flies were awful. They were everywhere and never gave me a moment's peace. But there was space, and we each received a clean cloth and some water and a rice ball.

My face was soon aflame from insect bites. I poured water on the cloth and put it on my face and let my aunt lead me. It took time to pick our way through all the people crowded on the floor, but at last she squeezed out a small space for our mats. I was a burden to her, I know, so young and immature. And here I was crying again: Isn't there anywhere else to go? It really smells here. I want to go home. I want to see my mother.

But she just rocked me in her arms. Nobody wants to be here, she said softly. Nobody wants to be here.

No one near us had any bedding; they just lay directly on the rutted floor, and they looked at my aunt with a strange eye when she unpacked our little cotton blankets. These were troubled, tormented people and they showed it in their ways of sleep. One thrashed about incessantly, turning from side to side and sometimes kicking me. Others cried or screamed in their dreams or else crept around the room at night, or simply lay there, exhausted, no matter what the fuss.

After we had slept and eaten rice again, we felt a little better, and my aunt talked to me of many things: of the war and the people who had starved or lost their houses and how they'd suffered great hardships, and of the men in Tokyo. I asked, as a child might, why these men made war when we couldn't even find my sister.

She smiled just a bit despite herself and helped me fix my hair. Their war is over now, she said. But ours is just beginning.

My aunt was desperate to find her husband and her son Hideki, and she went from shelter to shelter, or wherever she saw smoke from the piles of dead bodies they were burning, asking if anyone had seen them. But no.

Of my mother and family she said very little, but we prayed for them at night. People were always coming and going at our shelter. One time I saw a girl in the corner of the room who looked like my sister, leaning up against the wall. Save for her sparkling eyes, her whole face and arms were swathed in bandages. I knew in an instant that it wasn't Makiko, but still, I could feel her spirit lingering near me for many hours.

My aunt went over to the girl and asked about her family and whether she'd had any rice to eat. But the girl made no response. I tried not to look at her injuries or think of the pain she must be feeling. Gently, my aunt led her over to where our mats lay. Her face was so badly burnt she couldn't chew, so my aunt tore some of our dried sweet potato into strips and soaked it in water until it was soft enough for her to swallow.

I talked to her for a long time before I realized that the poor girl was deaf and blind. At last she lay down to sleep beside us and when I awoke the sun was already shining through the empty window frames.

I looked for the girl who looked like my sister, but she was gone. I'm sorry, my aunt said, but she died during the night. The soldiers had to come and take her away.

Grandfather's Treasure

Because Hon-chii was so far away, my cousin Hideki had spent many nights at our house after he started working at the steel factory. He was a mischievous boy and loved to play tricks on me, and I adored him for it. But the building where he'd worked was rubble now and not a soul was ever pulled from that shattered structure alive.

We went there again the following day. The police turned us away again, and so we walked on, to the ruins of my house, about half a mile from there.

I was determined to be of more help to my aunt this time; just the thought made me feel like a big girl, and it was a comfort to hear her say: I'm so grateful that you're with me, Hana-chan. You're all I have now, so please be a good girl. You must be careful. I don't know what I'd do if anything were to happen to you.

She didn't speak much after that. Both her sons were missing and her husband, too. What was there left to talk about?

When we finally got to the lot and saw again the blast pile that used to be my house, we lost our courage. For a long time my aunt just sat on a rock and did not move, as if she too were of stone. All day she sat like that. I have no memory of how I spent the time. When the sun bent low she rose and we walked in silence the five miles to the shelter.

We were back the next morning and started going through the burnt and powdery earth. Somehow my aunt had found a pair of gloves and a half-staff shovel. That helped: she didn't have to touch the stuff directly. There were nails and shards of glass everywhere and she picked her way carefully through it, shovel after shovel of horrid black ash. The work was hard and as she went about it, I heard her singing softly to herself.

Why are you digging, old fool? You know you won't find him here, not with that tool. So why are you digging, old fool?

She answered herself in a strange high voice. If I don't find his bones, and I only find stones, then he might be alive; he might be well.

The deeper she dug into the blast heap the more I wanted to

shovel too. Finally, after she removed all the heavy items and set aside what little she'd found of value, she relented and handed me the shovel.

I'd only been poking around in the charred earth for a few minutes when I touched something solid.

Must be another stone, my aunt said. I hope it's not a big one. But for once she was wrong.

Okaa-chan, I cried out, confusing her with my mother momentarily. I've found something. I think it's a jar.

It took us a long time to dig it out of the ground. It was indeed a jar of stone, black with soot and smaller and much heavier than I expected. We wiped it off as best we could, revealing traces of reddish brown. I remember my mother reading Aladdin and the Magic Lamp to me and for a moment my heart fluttered with expectation. Could it be true? Could it happen to me? I shook my silver *omamori*.

We got no magic wishes, no miracles. But we had some good luck nonetheless. My aunt pried the jar open. It was about as big as my head. To our surprise, she pulled out a package covered with an old yellow linen cloth. Inside it was a set of ivory miniatures— *netsuke*—carvings of the twelve animals of the Japanese zodiac.

Intrigued, I found the one of my sign, the white tiger. His eyes were sharp, and the mouth wide open. It reminded me of the picture in my grandfather's house: a samurai and a white tiger fighting in a bamboo grove.

What we'd found was my grandfather's treasure jar, and it contained things that would help us greatly in the coming months: a small box of rare stones shaped like animals and six *inro*—the small lacquer cases samurai used to hang from their sword sashes because they didn't have pockets.

Later we found broken rice bowls and fragments of the fine Imari plates my mother saved for important guests sticking out of the ground under what used to be the living room. How she loved her china, my mother. How sad she would have been to see her plates like this.

All day my aunt had been thinking about what to do with my

grandfather's treasure. The jar was too heavy to carry, and how would we ever keep the treasure safe, when there were so many desperate people on the streets and in our shelter?

Finally, she took a small jade dragon and put it in her pocket and together we buried the jar in a hole that we dug near the bone-dry pond.

That night when we got to the shelter, my uncle was there. He was so happy to see us that he burst into tears. Having him around was a huge relief to my aunt, even though he was often gone with his emergency work.

We went back to the house the next day, my aunt sifting through the ruins, looking for bones or anything that might be of value. But there wasn't much to find.

While she is working I drift off into what used to be our garden. The pine tree is still there, scorched and black and broken off halfway up the trunk. It is hot in the sun and I grow drowsy and fall into a waking dream. Makiko is with me again and we are playing hide and seek.

Ready or not, here I come, I call to her. Ready or not.

You can't find me.

Yes, I can, I answer. See? I found you easily. You can't hide from me.

Then from somewhere in the distance, I feel a warm breeze softly touch my hair. It is my turn to hide now and I go out behind our house and crawl beneath a big green bush. Makiko will never find me here.

But no one comes looking for me. I wait and I wait. Then I hear my mother's voice, calling me from the garden. Where are you? I cry.

I'm over here, my little Hana-chan. I'm over by the pond.

I run toward the sound of her sweet, familiar voice. The pond is full of lilies, and there are more pink princesses in the water than I've ever seen. The garden's green shimmers in the sunlight and reflects off the water in the pond.

But where are you, Okaa-chan? Okaa-chan, where are you?

After a while, my aunt comes and holds me gently in her arms.

She gives me water and some dry salted kelp. It tastes good and gradually I stop crying.

As we prepare to leave, two crows come circling high above us, black flowers riding the ill wind. I watch them for a long time, wondering where they'll go. There are no trees left to perch on, save for our broken char-black pine, and this they would not land on. They caw and caw accusingly and finally fly away.

My Aunt's Sons

For the next week we went from shelter to shelter, waiting in line at police stations, clinics, and emergency centers. We even went to see the mayor, but officials there told us the same thing we'd heard everywhere. No news. Sorry, very sorry.

We passed through a street lined on both sides with the shells of burnt-out buses. Is that the one my mother and I used to take? I asked. What if she and Sister were on it when the bomb was dropped?

You mustn't ask so many questions, my aunt said.

But what if we can't find them?

Then, we may have to give up at some point, she replied.

Maybe we'll find them tomorrow, I countered.

Maybe we will, little one, she said. Maybe we will.

After several days of futile searching, we set out for the countryside. As the road wound out of Hiroshima, the trees around us began to show signs again of greenery and life. It was wonderful to see colors again. I'd almost forgotten what they looked like.

I don't remember much about this period. The strangers were gone from the house and there was a lot to do to get it clean again.

My uncle was growing bald and he seemed discouraged. Some days he felt too sick to leave for work. No one knew what that might mean, so no one talked about it.

Throughout all this time, my aunt and uncle had had no news about either of their sons and they worried day and night. Hideki was just thirteen when the authorities compelled him to leave school and work in the steel factory. He cried bitterly about it at first, how he didn't want to work, that it was hard and dangerous, and that he wanted to go back to school. But what choice did he have?

Kenji was much older. I didn't know him very well, but everyone said that he was very smart and had a good physique. At seventeen he'd enlisted in the navy and was soon recruited into the *Tokubestu Kougeki-tai/Tokko-tai,* the Special Attack Forces. My uncle was very proud of him and he kept a picture of Kenji in his handsome uniform near the Flying Buddha shrine. But they seldom saw him once he began his training and now, since the spring, they had not heard a thing.

Some time that fall, a letter came to my aunt's house. It was from the War Ministry in Tokyo, forwarded to the village by the mayor of Hiroshima's office. I raced to my aunt to tell her the news.

You have a letter from Kenji. He's alive, I announced with great excitement. But at the sight of the envelope she just gasped and fell to her knees in agony.

My uncle took the letter from her hand and read:

Dear Mr. and Mrs. Takeda:
We deeply regret to inform you that Officer Kenji Takeda served his country with great honor and distinction in Okinawa.

That is all? my aunt asked. That's it?

They made him an officer, my uncle said with a mixture of pain and pride.

My aunt just shook her head, back and forth, back and forth. My uncle took another letter from the envelope.

This one is from Kenji, he said softly. It was written May 18.

Dear Father and Mother,
By the time you receive this letter, I will have already left on a special mission from which I cannot expect to return. Please forgive me for not coming to see you again. Please forgive the lack

of filial respect. Your faces have appeared to me again and again as I prepare for my glorious special mission. Please do not worry about me.

Sayonara,

Your proud son, Kenji

So that's what it means to be in the Special Forces, my aunt said through gritted teeth. They made him a kamikaze.

Uncle went to comfort her, but she just pushed him away.

Leave me alone, she snapped bitterly. I've lost my darling, Kenji. Where is the glory in that?

Little Nightingale

Every day I went to the Senkyo Temple to offer water and incense to my family and my ancestors, and every time my aunt would warn me to be careful. The streets of Hon-chii still harbored desperate people, their haunted, suspicious faces staring at me from down dim alleys.

There'd been a big typhoon that had hit in September, a torrent of thick, black rain that horrified people and downed many trees in our village and stripped the rest of their leaves. With that another wave of destitute people poured into a country town devoid of the means to help them.

Still, there'd been a kind of cleansing from the storm, for it seemed to wash the oil and soot from the air around Hiroshima, and the flooding waters lifted thousands of the dead out of the Motoyasu and carried them gently out to sea for burial.

I still imagined sometimes that my mother would come back, that I'd turn a corner somewhere and there she'd be. Oh, I know, I know, she was gone to the spirit world. All that was left of her here on earth were her glasses and that tiny box. We had taken it one day, my aunt and I, and given it to the temple. It would be safer there than in her home, she said.

I loved the smell of burning incense at the temple and the chance to be with my mother. But I felt closer to her spirit in the quiet of the temple garden than in the temple chamber, where they'd stuck her on a shelf along with a hundred other tiny boxes with their scraps of rice paper and Buddhist names inside. I still thought, because no one had found her body, not even a bone, perhaps she was not really dead. How could you be sure? No, I didn't believe it, I didn't want to believe it, because I knew they could never fit my mother in that box.

Uncle died sometime that fall. I don't remember the day, but I do remember going with my aunt to pray for him at the Senkyo Temple graveyard. It was raining and the monk who prayed for us had no umbrella, so we gave him ours while he chanted a sutra to the soggy ground.

It must have been horrible for my aunt. But still, what I remember the most about that time was the mosquitoes. Those miserable things are always the last creatures to die in the fall. They outlive the people, they outlive the flowers, and they outlive the falling leaves, and as we pray for my poor uncle they feast on me. If I could only find a frog, for there were many in the pond, I would tie him to my leg with a string so he could eat the horrid things. But when I began hopping around during the service, my aunt gave me a sharp tap on the back of the head.

It was odd about mosquitoes, though. I'd noticed that whenever they landed on someone's burns, which they did with great frequency that fall, that person never felt an itch. Their pain was just too strong. That's what my aunt told me.

The longer I stayed at the temple the more I found myself drawn to the Kannon statue. There was something about her face, her calm expression, that was very reassuring, much more so than the pinched, pained faces I saw wherever else we went. The monks said that she was a Bosatu, a Bodhisattva, and that she came with Lord Amida to take worthy souls to Pure Land.

I asked if that meant my mother was in Pure Land, too. The younger one, the one who had chanted sutra for my uncle, frowned, but the older man smiled a bit and his kind eyes lit up, and he said yes, that's exactly where she'd gone.

I tried to find comfort in that. And so I went and knelt before the Kannon goddess and asked her many things: about bombs and tiny boxes, about dragonflies, and men with no hands, and others dying when their hair fell out, and what was I supposed to do until I too could go to Pure Land? My questions did not annoy her, not the way they annoyed my aunt, and bit by bit, it seemed, she began to smile at me.

I went home and told my aunt about the Kannon goddess's smile, but she had little time for me now, for her own time was approaching. A child is about to be born, she put it sharply, without a father, without her brothers, in the midst of all this. I pity the poor thing. So I went back to the Kannon goddess and talked to her again, and again I saw her smile.

After that I visited her every time I could. I looked for her in the morning and when I went to sleep, for in her face, or so it seemed to me, I could see my mother, smiling down on me from Pure Land.

Despite her condition, or perhaps to avoid thinking about it, my aunt spent hours every day at the emergency clinic they'd set up in the temple's wide hall. I would wake up early to help her with the cleaning and boiling water. I was used to wandering among the burnt and wounded now, bringing them clean water or fresh bandages and sometimes fanning them to keep the heat and flies away. I tried to speak to each of them, the way my mother had taught me: Good morning, sir. Good morning, madam. How are you today? Do you feel hot? Would you like some water?

Then suddenly a tortured voice called out. Oh, wanton war, waster of men, why have we done this to ourselves?

Fool, an angry voice retorted, it was the Americans. We didn't bomb ourselves.

Oh, yes we did, the first screamed.

No, no, it was the Military Police, the *Kempei-tai,* another shouted. They got us into this.

My sons gave their lives for the Emperor, a third one yelled. Don't you dare say a word against them.

Oh, I dare, the first one raged. I dare to tell the truth.

And what is that? a fourth one snarled.

I'll tell you, the angry man said. From the very first second those geniuses in Tokyo decided to attack Pearl Harbor, Japan was doomed. We might as well have attacked ourselves and saved everyone the time.

No! No! You're a liar, a traitor, the others shouted and they rushed on the poor man and began to choke him.

I was scared and ran to the other room and there I came upon a young man who had lost his leg. He was still wearing a faded army uniform, perhaps he had no other clothes, and when he saw me, he rose on one elbow to speak.

Well, what do we have here? he asked with a warm, welcoming smile. A little Florence Nightingale?

And so I became his Nightingale-san. I rang my silver *omamori* and sang for him, and he told me about the great nurse and what she had done to heal the sick and wounded in some other war.

She was kind, like you, Hana-chan, the young man said. That's why we call a good nurse Angel in White.

I visited him several times after that and listened to his stories about Thomas Edison and a wonderful doctor called Seishu Hanaoka who had saved the lives of many patients. The young man had been studying medicine before the war, but now, he wondered, how could he ever become a doctor?

But can't you be a one-legged doctor? I asked and I hopped around like a silly stork.

Perhaps I can, my little Nightingale-san, he said with a laugh. And when I become a doctor, you shall be my nurse.

It's curious, but I still remember his words. They've stayed in my memory all these years. And I did become a nurse.

My aunt gave birth in her own house just as the days were at their shortest. I heard her cries of pain, but when the midwife finally let me see her, she looked very happy and relieved. The baby was a girl, her first. The neighbors celebrated the healthy birth with what few supplies they had.

As soon as I saw her, I loved my new cousin, loved looking at her sweet little face and talking to her, at her bedside every morning and evening.

I'm your big sister, I used to whisper to her. We can play together when you get older and I will teach you many things. Her hands and feet, everything about her, were so small and loveable that even her crying didn't bother me. Soon I was pestering my aunt to let me hold her, and I sang to her and handled her as often as my aunt would let me. And then just as a wondrous bright little person was emerging from its first weeks of helpless infancy, the baby caught a cold, and perhaps because we had no heat, it turned to pneumonia and a high fever and after several days of suffering she died.

After that, my aunt withdrew ever more tightly into herself. She used to be a cheerful woman, with a friendly smiling face. But after the baby died, her smile died too. She became strict with me and hardly ever gave me praise, much as I craved it. It was only later, much, much later, that I finally understood her better, when I thought of all she'd lost and how hard she had to work to raise me.

CHAPTER THREE

The Blue Sky Club

Winter had been hard beyond all reckoning. Food was short, there was hardly any heat, and then in February, while we were away at the temple, the house was robbed and everything my aunt had owned was stolen. My poor aunt; I don't know how she managed to carry on. We stayed with some neighbors for a while and then moved to a wooden hut in Hiroshima. This barracks house, as they called it, was a cramped and shabby place, but we did have a kerosene stove and there was donated barley at times, and a roof that kept the rain out unless it really poured.

This latter was a constant headache to my aunt. She was always adding pieces of wood and zinc to it that had blown off other people's houses or anything else we could find. But there was never a good way to secure it all, and every time there was a strong wind, some of the pieces blew away. Then one night a violent storm blew in and everything flew off in a great clattering racket. After that, we called it the Blue Sky Club, because when we looked up, that is all we saw.

My Mother's Warm Hands

Somehow they had managed to open the Honkawa Elementary School during the winter. I didn't really want to go at first, but my aunt insisted on it. She practically dragged me there the first few weeks. The roads, those that were free of debris, were covered with

51

mud and pools of murky, standing water. The school itself was a shell, three floors without a window or a door and a basement full of wreckage and water. Everything that was made of wood had been vaporized. Only the metal and concrete remained. Yet somehow the parents had made it clean.

Even before we got there, I sensed my sister's spirit. But no, it was not her spirit I felt but my own longing, for she was nowhere that I looked, and then I had to remind myself, again, that spirits had no substance, that there was nothing they could do. Perhaps that was why they wandered and why I still looked for her every time I walked on Honkawa Avenue.

The first day of school was a great commotion. Children were streaming in from all directions. Some had a parent or an older sister; some came with their cousins or their aunts. Everyone had to stop at the entrance and take off his shoes and put them in the big rack along the wall. A lot of the kids had no shoes at all. I could see that their feet were all red and sore. Some of the others were wearing *wara-zori,** sandals of thick matted straw. I was one of the lucky ones: I had a pair of *geta** shoes, wooden clogs my aunt had managed to find somehow. They were too big, but at least they kept my feet dry, as long as I stayed out of mud puddles.

My aunt looked down at the floors she had gone on her hands and knees to scrub and she grumbled like a woman who knew the contours of the concrete floor far too well.

How will you students keep the classroom clean? she asked. Look at them; already they're tracking in mud.

I don't think she expected a response and I gave her none. It was usually easier that way.

Although I did not know it then—I was too young to see much beyond myself—there were many children like me, others who had had lost their entire families. But I didn't think much of them. I spent my time envying the ones like Midori, who would come hand in hand with her mother almost every day to school.

She was the one I resented the most. I would watch in secret while her mother talked to her sweetly, holding her hand or touching her cheek or pulling back her hair as she changed into her school shoes. Nobody else had school shoes. And nobody else had a mother like that either, and oh, how I ached for my own.

Then one day, her mother approached me, smiling warmly.

Hello! I am Midori's mother. Do you know her? I came with her today.

How do you do, I replied formally, bowing stiffly.

She smiled again and went to take my hand and walk with me to the classroom, but I could only pull away, determined to go alone. What I wanted, of course, was what I could not have: my mother's two warm hands, touching me, patting my cheek or stroking my hair.

But with spring comes the sun, and school soon became the most enjoyable thing about my life. I had friends to play with, and there was a small shelf in a corner of the room with books on it, thanks to a few parents, such as Midori's, who had been able to save some during the war.

It was my mother who had started me reading. I often thought of her, the way she would hold me on her lap while she read to me, and how I would look up at her and see my reflection in her glasses, and when I found some stories that we had read together—The Old Man Who Could Make Flowers Bloom from Ashes, The Moon Princess, The Crane's Repayment—I wanted to read them over and over. But there were so few books at school that we were not allowed to take any home.

That first year everyone was crowded into the same room. It was the only one deemed safe enough. Mr. Kato, a stern man, especially with the boys, was in charge of the older pupils, even though he was new to teaching.

Miss Yamada, a young woman with a pretty face, was my teacher; she had charge of the lower grades. With all the commotion of competing lessons, it was easy to get distracted, and we sometimes got lessons from the older kids after school. But they talked a lot about ghosts, too, the ones that lived in the basement, and we were terrified to go down there.

It was coming home from school that spring that I saw the first *tetsudo gusa* shoots. My aunt let me walk home alone now, if I

Children with Miss Yamada, in front of Honkawa School. (Courtesy of Honkawa Elementary School, Hiroshima)

promised to come directly, and I was going very carefully, so as not to get mud on the new tunic she had sewed me, when I saw them.

The bright green shoots fascinated me. I bent down to feel the plant, to study it the way Makiko had taught me. Its leaves gave off a faint grassy smell, but could we eat it? I ran home to tell my aunt. Everyone had said that nothing would ever grow in this ground again, that it would be seventy-five years before anything came up, and yet here they were, fresh and green and new this spring. After that, she told me that whenever I could find any *tetsudo gusa*, I should pull it out by the roots and take it home so that she could put it in the rice or make it into gruel.

Shortly after that my aunt decided to move us to my family's property. It was going to take a lot of work. The reason, she told me, was so that I would be closer to the Honkawa School when it started up again.

That much is true. But I found out later she had another reason. She needed Grandfather's treasure jar, for the money she'd gotten for the *inro* and the precious stones was long gone and she dared not dig when anyone might see or hear her. There were thieves everywhere, and it was dangerous to reveal any sign of wealth.

It had been months since I had seen the neighborhood they called the A-Bomb Zone. That was not a term that any of us liked. Most of the streets were clear now. There'd been some help from the *gaijin*—the Aussies and Americans—and most of the rubble had been removed.

To our relief, the concrete blocks we'd piled up to mark the edges of our property were still in place. We'd stacked ours well above sufficient height, and people had respected them. With the help of a few neighbors, we worked all day and into the night to clear away debris, my aunt as always going through it with a country woman's eye and sorting things in piles.

The next day we pulled apart our barracks house and loaded it piece by jagged piece into my uncle's cart. We walked it all the way to our property, and after several trips and the help of our new neighbors, my aunt hammered our new barracks house together, directly over the spot where the treasure jar was buried. Where she got the hammer and nails or the skill to use them, I do not know, but the house she eventually cobbled together was bigger and warmer than the one we'd had, and the Honkawa School was not far away.

Akiko

A few hardy birds, sparrows and crows for the most part, had returned with the hot weather, and they chirped and cawed sometimes as if they hadn't a care in the world. Despite many fine days that summer, there was little joy in people's lives. Grim-faced silence ruled the streets and held the city in its angry grip.

Almost a year had passed since the bomb. My aunt took a job at a garbage-collection site and worked there every day from early morning until late at night. The fall term would be starting again in September and she worried about leaving me alone. That is why Akiko came into my life. She was in the fifth grade and lived with her cousins in a barracks house not far from us.

One day one of her cousins took us to a temple to pay homage to their ancestors. It was a few kilometers beyond the A-Bomb Zone, not far from the Gokoku Shrine. Above us we could see trees in the mountains. It seemed a magical place; everything was green. But even at the temple there were birds and, in a field nearby, honeybees busily working a small patch of white cosmos flowers. These were the first flowers we'd seen of any kind. For some reason only the white ones were blooming and we raced out to look at them.

Why was that? I asked Akiko. Why aren't there any pink cosmos flowers?

I don't know, she replied. Perhaps the white ones are the reincarnation of all the people who died that day.

Akiko was an active girl and when her cousin went off to pray, it wasn't long before we started playing leapfrog. Somehow I fell and cut my knee. It hurt, not enough to cry, but I guess I wanted some attention and I ran to her for comfort. For a time we just held each other. Then she saw the blood on my leg and she screamed so suddenly that I was terrified.

Why, oh why, oh why?

It's okay, I said. It doesn't really hurt that much. I tried to console her, but she couldn't hear me.

Oh why, oh why, oh why? she cried. There were so many of them. They're lying everywhere, on the ground, in the road. They're moaning, groaning, screaming, Help me; help me. But . . . I couldn't help them. I couldn't even help them. Bodies . . . there were bodies everywhere. I saw a man. His arm was blown off . . . it was lying next to him. Oh Hanako . . .

We were back in that day, the day the bomb took the color away from every living thing. Her class had been sent to cut grass at the old Gokoku Shrine. It was only by chance that she'd been standing behind the Torii Gate.

It was like a hundred typhoons, she wailed, a blinding light, an exploding wind. . . . It knocked me over. I thought I'd died. . . . Everything went black. I was on my stomach, on the road. I couldn't see; I couldn't hear; I couldn't understand. My leg was

A Hiroshima family at the Torii Gate, a month before the bombing. (Courtesy of Toshimi Ishida)

cut and I was bleeding. What had happened? Had I been struck by lightning?

There were people screaming, crying, pleading in their pain. There were so many of them, so many people lying there. Who were these people? What had happened? But that was what saved me, Hanako—the Torii Gate.

My head ached so badly I couldn't think. I didn't know what to do. It was only when I finally could stand up that I saw . . . the whole city was burning, Hanako. The whole city was on fire! You could hear it crackle. I . . . I couldn't . . . I didn't know what to do. I was so afraid. Where were my friends, my teachers; where were my classmates? I tried to find them; I tried so hard to find someone that I knew. But they were gone, gone; everyone was gone. I didn't know what to do, Hanako. I didn't know what to do. Why were all those people lying on the street?

Then I heard them. They were moaning and chanting, a whole long file of them, coming slowly toward me. Ahhh—

Oh, please, Akiko, don't talk about the *yurai* ghosts, I pleaded with her. But she could not hear me.

The way they were dragging themselves, Hanako . . . There were carts full of bodies. I saw some people walking with them. I wanted to speak to them. Maybe they could tell me what to do. But no one said a word, Hanako. There was nothing but their chanting and the awful wailing. I was so afraid. I . . . I wanted to get away, but they were watching me.

No, Akiko, don't talk about it, I pleaded, but she went on anyway.

I began to run to them. One of them saw me, and he beckoned me to join him. He had no skin on his hands, Hanako. His skin was hanging off him in strips. He reached out and tried to grab me, but I jumped back, and then he pointed at me with his bony, bloody fingers and kept walking on. I didn't know what to do, Hanako. I didn't know what to do, and so I started running after them again.

I tried to plug my ears, but she turned and looked full at me.

I don't know how it happened, she said quietly, but somehow I heard a tiny voice, calling to me from the Torii Gate: Sister, oh Sister, please help. Please help me.

It was a little girl of four or five. There was blood all over her little tunic. I remember her dark eyes; they were racing back and forth and her hands and legs were twitching. Her back was all burnt; it was terrible. I wanted to help her. I just wanted to help her, that is all.

I didn't know what to do, so I lifted her on my back and I tried to run after them. I wanted to be part of them, yes; I wanted to follow them, up to the mountains, away from the fire and my terrible headache and all those horrid bodies lying on the ground. So I took her with me.

But they wouldn't wait for me, Hanako. My leg was hurt and my head was spinning. She was just too heavy for me. I had to put her down. I called to them, but they wouldn't wait. They'd lost their spirits, Hanako. They couldn't hear and they couldn't talk. They just went on and on, moaning and groaning up the road toward the mountains. I tried to keep up with them. I tried. But they wouldn't wait. They couldn't wait for me.

And then they were gone and we were all alone. My hair, where she'd touched it, was all clotted and covered with blood. It was thick and sticky and horrible. I looked at the girl. I reached for her hand. There was a little response, a tiny squeeze, and then . . . nothing. Nothing I did made any difference.

I put her down softly and sat down beside her. A man came by. I asked him what to do. But he was bleeding, bleeding from the eyes, and he just walked on by me blindly, as if I weren't there. Down the road, I could hear someone, a man I think. He was calling for water. He was desperate, screaming for help: Water. Oh please, gimme water. Ohplease, ohplease, ohplease. But there was no one to give him any. Everyone was gone.

I don't know why, but the sound of his voice seemed to wake me and then he saw me; he started calling to me. Come, little girl; come to me. I wanted to help him, Hanako, but I was so afraid. He kept lunging at me, but he was stuck to the ground. He couldn't get up. I started running. I wanted to go home so badly. I tried to get there, Hanako. I tried so many times, took all the roads I knew. But the fire was everywhere. It was so hot, I couldn't . . . I tried to get there, I tried so hard, but I couldn't. The fire was just too hot.

She stopped now, mastering her tears, and a determined look came across her face that I had not seen before. But I could still talk about things then, and I asked about her mother. I knew it was wrong the moment I asked. She shook her head sadly and bit her lip and then burst into tears again. I leaned my head against her shoulder, and together we wept until our grief gave out. And that's how Akiko and I became sisters.

Red Fire

My aunt had taken it into her head that she should scold me frequently. For a long time I thought it was because she didn't like me, that I was a burden. There was so little rice and hardly a cloth to make a blanket for winter, and here I'd grown two inches in a year and had to have new clothes for school. No matter what I did, it always seemed to displease her.

If she had only tried to talk to me, perhaps I might have understood. But she couldn't anymore; she was barely hanging on. I couldn't see that then.

One incident proves a point about her. It's how I know she loved me, even though I could never get her to say so. It must have been toward the end of summer. She'd asked me to keep an eye on the fire while she ran some errand, but I forgot myself and went out to play with some friends, for people were coming back to Hiroshima and others were moving in, and so there were children again.

It was only when I heard the angry shouting that I remembered the *konro* stove. I'd left it burning, run off without thinking, and now, somehow the charcoal had started a fire. A man in the barracks house next door saw the smoke and came rushing over to put it out. He was not a happy man, and by the time I raced back he was cursing my aunt and threatening to drive us off the property.

How dare you put us all at risk like that? he yelled furiously. Aren't things hard enough? You can burn yourselves down and who would care? But you could have burned up this whole barracks with everybody in it. How dare you let a child tend a fire?

Then he turned on me. All that I have in this world, the few things I still possess, are what I carried on my back all the way from Osaka. And you want to burn them? You want to burn this whole place down? Well, haven't you seen enough burn, you stupid peasants?

My aunt, who had been bowing her regret with deep dignity, stiffened at the insult and then drew herself up, took a deep breath, and apologized again with all the grace left in her.

I was wrong; please forgive me. She's such a small girl, too small to keep a fire. Please forgive me.

Finally, the man sulked off. I knew that I'd made a very bad mistake, and I was afraid of what my aunt would do. She was as strong as a horse and several times had come within an inch of slapping me. But this time she said nothing, just clenched her teeth and let out a great slow breath and told me:

Hanako! You must make *gassho*.* Apologize before your ancestors. Promise that you will never take your eyes off the fire again.

And when I'd gone to the temple, sat *seiza*-style to show respect, apologized to my ancestors, and promised not to fail in my duty again, Aunt bought me a piece of rock candy on the way home.

I had seen the GIs in their Jeeps, passing out candy and chewing gum, but my aunt had always forbidden me to take anything from them. So I savored that rock candy. I held it in my cheek and sucked it so long I got the hiccups, and then I squatted down on my hams and pretended to be a frog, hiccupping all the way home. My aunt didn't smile much, but I could see that she was amused by my antics, as much as she allowed herself to be, so I croaked and hicked all the louder.

She never referred to the fire after that. But whenever circumstances forced her to be elsewhere and I had to watch the *konro* stove, some adult from the barracks always came to check on me.

I used to go with my aunt to help her in the empty lot where she and some neighbor women were trying to grow vegetables, especially sweet potatoes, using seeds she'd brought from her village. It had cost my grandfather's ivory zodiac to buy the tools, and two weeks of constant labor to clear the land and get the hard-baked earth ready to receive our seed, but now that we had planted, there were many hungry eyes watching our garden grow.

We came every evening to pull weeds and watch for thieves. The gangs of boys were the worst, teenagers and even younger sometimes, quick and sly as foxes.

All summer the women kept their watch, their shovels at the ready. Two years of home defense training at the temple and another year spent surviving the bomb had made them as hard as the earth itself; no mere boy was going to be a match for them.

But there were some lighter times, too. Once I was prowling around the rocks at the edge of our field when I came upon a very curious plant. It was an ashen, spindly thing but green enough when you blew the dust off. That was interesting enough. But beneath the leaves there was a little pod. It was shiny and red and it looked like a bean.

But was it? How could I be sure? What would Aunt say? It could be poison. But who'd ever heard of a poison bean?

Three times I walked away from that bright red bean, and three times my craving for it grew. At last I can stand it no more. I've been so hungry for so long, I pick it. My aunt, who misses nothing, looks up from her weeding, and out of the corner of my eye I see her coming. She makes to say something, but before she can, I pop it whole into my mouth and bite down hard.

Aah! An explosion: my mouth's on fire; my nose is running; tears are pouring from my eyes. My aunt starts to smile and then, as I shout and hop about, she begins to laugh. Perhaps I had never seen her laugh. But now she is laughing so hard there are tears in her eyes, and the sound of her laughter starts me laughing too.

Now you know what a red pepper tastes like, she says, her face wreathed in a lively smile.

Now I know what a firecracker tastes like, I reply.

An older woman, one of the ones who works the field with us, has been watching and is having a good laugh, too.

Firecracker? You are our firecracker, little Hana-chan, she says. You light up our sky. It's that silver *omamori* your mother gave you. May its good luck always be with you.

CHAPTER FOUR

An Organ on His Back

The summer was ending and it was time to attend Honkawa School again. Thirteen months had passed since the bomb they called Little Boy* was dropped. The school had been well within the impact zone, and if nobody talked about that, it was because nobody needed to. The results were everywhere: the broken walls; the empty window frames; the lame, the maimed, the disabled children.

But we were used to all that by now. At least there were other kids around. We had our share of fun. One morning just as I was taking off my outdoor shoes, I heard some of the boys shouting.

Look, one of them cried. It was Koichi, ever on the alert, leaning way out of the empty window. It's Sensei. And he's got something really big strapped to his back.

What is it? another boy asked.

It's got keys on it, Koichi shouted, like an organ.

An organ on his back? No one could believe that.

Look, everyone. He's coming.

Then the whole class ran toward the window. An organ you could carry on your back? No one had seen anything like that before.

Kato Sensei walked up in the courtyard. Get away from that window, he commanded the children who were threatening to push each other out the second-floor window in their excitement. Be careful! Boys! Come and help me! They all rushed downstairs, we girls not far behind them, and surrounded the new curiosity.

What is it? Where did it come from? The questions came flying.

Mr. Kato was the youngest teacher in the school. Four years in
military school and two more in the navy during the war had made
him a hard man. And yet he had a soldier's sense of honor—he
was fair—and it was this quality, I think, that made the children
like him despite his severity.

Where did you get it, Sensei?

On the other side of the river.

How, Sensei?

I borrowed it from another school.

And you carried it all the way on your back?

Hai!

And can you play it, Kato Sensei? Can you play the organ?

No.

Well, then, who can?

I can, came a voice from behind us.

We all looked back. It was the new teacher, Miss Takahashi,
the one with the burns on her face. We knew that she had studied
opera in Tokyo and when she sang, her voice could make the
skies turn blue and the birds fall silent in admiration. It purified
our spirits to hear her. But what sorrow hid behind that voice, that
we could not know, for no opera company would take a woman
with a face like that, no matter how beautifully she sang.

Many people assumed she was a *hibakusha,* a word already
being used to describe the people who'd survived the bomb. But
she always denied that and said it was the result of an automobile
accident she'd had when she was at the conservatory in Tokyo.
Whatever the truth, to be called a *hibakusha* was a nasty, malicious
thing, for an odor of fear and exclusion clung to the word, and if
there's one thing the Japanese fear, it's exclusion.

There were several children who were clearly *hibakusha* in my
class and there were others, like Midori, who were clearly not. Her
family had been in the mountains during the war, away from the
cities and their bombs, and hence they were able to keep most of
their possessions—like their books. And then there were children
like me. I didn't want to be a *hibakusha,* I knew that much. But of
course that is precisely what I was.

Still, I was strong and healthy, while dozens of my classmates had lost an arm or leg or were badly scarred by burns. Remembering such things is hard, but hiding them can be even harder on you.

For a while we worked at the school, my aunt and I. How she found the time I don't know, but I remember her, gaunt, grim-faced, indomitable, wrapping and unwrapping bandages in stoic, stolid silence. It sticks, blood, when it's on the cloth too long, and with burn victims it is always a slow and careful business. I had gotten so that I was almost as good as she at never tearing new flesh. You have to be generous with the water and precious ointments and very, very careful. You get to know people that way, too. You talk with them and they tell you many stories. Any nurse can tell you that.

Hibakusha kids did not play with the others very much. Only during music did they join us, and then some of them sang with great joy and abandon.

Takahashi Sensei, with her beautiful voice and the way she played the little organ, taught us many songs and poems. And every other week Mr. Kato would walk out of the schoolyard with the organ on his back and take it across the river to the school from which he borrowed it.

I could sing like a crow and when I wanted to make the *hibakusha* kids laugh I used my crow's voice and hopped around flapping my wings, but Miss Yamada caught me and after that I had to stop. Miss Takahashi didn't seem to mind my antics, for I liked to recite those old poems, and I loved to listen to her voice. I still remember the words to a poem by Kenji Miyazawa* for which she wrote the music. *We beat the rain. We beat the wind, summer's heat, and winter's snow.*

One of the *hibakusha* girls had a glorious voice, so much sweeter than mine or anybody else's in the class that she was Miss Takahashi's favorite. She seemed like a nice girl, but her side was all burned and then she got sick and we didn't see her after that. No one knew just why, but there was talk in the air that there was something wrong with Hiroshima.

We were only just learning a new word: radiation. What did it mean? No one seemed to know. Perhaps Kato Sensei did, but fear comes like silence in the night, and no one had the courage to ask him directly.

At that time, people thought radiation was contagious, that it was a kind of malignancy you could pass on to your children. No one wanted to marry anyone from Hiroshima for fear that their children would be subject to genetic mutation. It was thought that even touching a *hibakusha* might make you sick. Imagine such cruel, blind ignorance. How can I tell you, friend, how easy it is to waste a life?

My aunt and I were no different, it hurts me now to confess. If it was normal that I shunned the *hibakusha* then, it is surely shameful to me now.

One day my aunt stopped coming to the school to help nurse the *hibakusha* kids. Neither she nor anyone else ever said a word about it, but my days as a young Nightingale were coming to an end.

Mud-Ball Dreams

One night, when she thought no one would hear us, my aunt and I dug up Grandfather's treasure jar, and she took the last of the precious stones. Where she went with them, I do not know, but when she came back it was late at night, and for a while we had white rice and even a little watermelon to eat. Even that I felt guilty about, and I told none of my classmates, even Midori. Then the rice ran out and that was the last time we tasted much more than plain fare for many months.

Still, it is no crime to be poor when your neighbors are poor, too.

Slowly, the parents were cleaning out the other classrooms at the Honkawa School. My aunt was still willing to do that, working without stop for hours at a time, removing the broken blackboards and disassembled bookshelves, hauling the shattered shoe racks and splintered desks down the crumbling, broken stairway and out of the building, and putting a few choice pieces for our barracks house to one side.

Honkawa School classroom, 1946. (Courtesy of Honkawa Elementary School, Hiroshima)

It wasn't until they'd cleaned out the burnt-out room in the basement, the ghost room as we called it, that anyone dared go down there. As for me, I much preferred the playground.

Our teacher, Miss Yamada, was full of surprises. We had so few books that she was constantly looking for ways to keep us learning. The day of the Harvest Moon, she took us down to the riverbank. It was a wonderful clear day and the autumn sun warmed us until a kind of lazy reverie settled over us all.

Now, everybody, today is *Otsukimi,* when we celebrate the Harvest Moon, she said in her gentle voice. Let's all find some clay or mud and shape it into *odango* dumplings, so we can make our offerings to Princess Moon for a rich rice harvest.

The more she talked of dumplings, the more I yearned for the ones Grandmother used to make, the way they smelled and how they felt in your mouth all chewy and tangy. And I thought of the ones she'd made for me the last time I saw her, and of the food she'd made for other full-moon nights—white rice, dried sardines, vegetable sushi wrapped in seaweed, even hard-boiled eggs sometimes—and how my sister and I used to set them out on the windowsill. We'd wait until the sun went down and the full-faced moon appeared before we'd eat. The dumplings always tasted better then, for there was magic in the full moon, or so Grandmother used to say, and you could surely taste it in her *odango*.

Miss Yamada's gentle voice washed over us troubled children and soon we were lying on our backs, eyes to the drifting clouds. Time was healing us, she could see it working slowly through its stages, and a day along the river, listening to the rippling water flow, could only help it on its course.

Kazuko wasn't making dumplings but a fish as big as she was. Oh my, Miss Yamada said, what kind of fish is that? It looks delicious.

This is a sea bream, Kazuko replied. It brings good fortune. What do you think? Should I grill it, or should I boil it?

Oh no, that would be bad luck, Yamada Sensei joked. We should save it for the festival next week. Otherwise Lord Ebisu* might be offended.

No, he will not, Kazuko answered with great authority. A fish this big must be eaten while it's fresh. Lord Ebisu is a fisherman; he will understand.

I hadn't tasted fish for a long, long time and so I puckered up and made a fish face at her. Next to me, Midori looked up, licked her lips with an infectious smile, then went back to patting the light-brown mud into delicious fish balls.

Most of the boys in the class had started out making the usual boy things—cars and boats and planes—Koichi, of course, had made a Jeep—but then they too seemed to fall under the spell of Yamada Sensei's voice and the warm afternoon sun and the gentle rippling of the swift but fishless Motoyasu, and bit by bit the sharp edges of their machines softened and began to take the shape of fish and fruits and other foods they had not tasted in a long time.

Oh, grapes, one boy said, looking at Midori's fish balls. Cold grapes.

Which kind, another asked, the red or green?

The purple are the best, a third one chimed in.

No, no, still another boy replied, chilled melon balls are better.

You're all wrong. Cold tomatoes are the best, Koichi said, as if he'd just eaten them.

Cold tomatoes? I asked. When did you have them?

This summer, he said emphatically.

How could that be, we all wanted to know, cold tomatoes in the summer? Even Teacher lent an ear.

It was like this, Koichi said, pleased as always to be the center of attention. My dad got some ice—

Ice? we repeated incredulously. Where did he find ice in the summertime?

From the Americans, he said matter-of-factly. They have a big icemaking machine and so much ice they sometimes dump it in the sea.

Now this was even more incredible: so much ice in the summer that they would dump it in the sea?

But how did he get it? Sensei wanted to know. You can't just go up to an American and ask him for ice, can you?

That's what my father did, he said with a certain pride in his voice. He's a fisherman, you know, and fishermen need ice, especially if you're after tuna. And you can't find them unless you go way out into the Far Sea.

The Far Sea, we repeated with wonder. Your father goes fishing there?

Sure, Koichi said. He does it all the time. Only in this case, he took some of the ice and put it on the tomatoes.

Tomatoes, several children repeated longingly. Where did he get them?

From the Americans.

Wasn't he afraid?

No, not at all. He traded some fish for the tomatoes and some ice and then he put them in the freezer—

A freezer? What was that? Would Koichi's stories never end?

A freezer is a box that's got copper on the inside. You put ice in it and it keeps everything cold.

Even in the summer?

Especially in the summer, Koichi said proudly. That's how we ate cold tomatoes. Ah, he said triumphantly, they were so delicious.

I remembered my grandmother used to put gourds in the well to chill them, but I'd never seen a freezer box with copper lining on the inside. Do you have one in your house? I asked.

No, he said. But my dad has one on his boat. When I grow up, I'm going to be a fisherman, too. I'll go to the Far Sea and fill my freezers with so much tuna that no one ever has to go hungry again.

Then I will be your wife, Kazuko said suddenly. Then I can eat all the fish and cold tomatoes I want.

But that was too much for Koichi. I'll never marry anyone, he said with a shy smile and skipped away.

Teru-Teru-Bozu

My aunt was always working. There was never a moment when she took the time to read a book or tell a story or take me to the countryside to visit our ancestors or just to see some flowers and green trees. Most of the little conversation we shared focused on food and the chores I had to do in our community garden or around the barracks house. It was getting colder now as the winter approached, and I could see why she had taken so many of the school's broken old desks and chairs and piled them in our garden—firewood.

Only at school did I have a chance to be a child, so I went happily almost every day. But many children would not come on rainy days. One of the reasons was that the roof leaked in many places, so that we were constantly moving our orange-crate chairs to drier spaces. Often when it rained there was hardly a spot where you could avoid the water dripping on your head, so that it was almost impossible to study. Of course, this did not displease everyone, and if by some chance Mr. Kato was not around, the boys made sure that nothing constructive could get done.

One day, after a particularly long spell of rain, Miss Yamada suggested we make *teru-teru-bozu*. These are little dolls that you hang from the windows to wish for fine weather. My aunt had been bringing rags home from the collection site where she worked with the hope of accumulating enough to make us blankets for the winter, and it took me a long time to convince her to give me some, but when I got to school, I had more rags than anybody else, so I felt quite proud of that.

It was Akiko who suggested that we hang one *teru-teru-bozu* for each member of our family who had passed away during the war, and without a word we all agreed. We children never talked about these things, not in school, but today, for one day, it seemed we could. One of my classmates had to make fifteen *teru-teru-bozu*, and when I was finished with my five, I helped him make two of them.

I remember the feeling of the day better than the details. We'd put all the crate chairs together in a circle, toward the middle of the room. There was only an occasional bit of water that leaked on you there, save for that which dripped from a curious set of stalactites that had formed on the ceiling. When they finally released a drop of water, it always fell on your head and splattered loudly enough that the boys, ever on the prowl for mischief and amusement, would hear it and laugh at you.

After the rags and bits of cloth had been washed and dried, we colored our *teru-teru-bozu*. Kazuko had three. She'd put a stamp on each of their robes, and a little picture of Buddha on the back of the one for her mother, using a paste that Yamada Sensei had made.

Midori, who had only one doll—and that not family but only a distant cousin—drew a pretty face on hers. How I wanted to have a pen like that, one that could draw faces in ink. I could hold it, of course, as Midori was my friend, but her mother had told her in no uncertain terms that no one but she was to make characters with the pen. Ink was just too expensive.

But we had clay from the river in varying shades of brown and grey and Miss Takahashi had brought old *meisen monpe**
trousers and some tailor's scissors to school, so we cut them up

and everyone got a piece. Mine had part of a yellow flower on it, with threads of green and blue.

Soon there was a string of *teru-teru-bozu* dolls running the whole length of the classroom and when the wind blew through the empty windows, they danced and fluttered and threatened to fly off.

But even now, when I think of those *teru-teru-bozu* again, dancing brightly along the window tops, I have no wish to go further and draw from that deep well of memory the exact recollection of the ones I made for my mother and the others.

We watched each other and counted the dolls our friends made and grieved, each in our own way. They say crying can be good for you. I don't know. I cried a lot that afternoon. We were not stupid; we could count each other's loss. By the end of the day, 157 *teru-teru-bozu* were hanging from the string.

I wondered about Koichi, too. He made three dolls out of old newspaper and had put a blue ribbon on two of them. The other had an intricate silver ring around it, fashioned from the shiny foil wrapping around some American chewing gum. I wanted to ask him about this third one, but he was always joking and never let me close enough to find the answer.

I often looked up at the *teru-teru-bozu*, and it seemed as if they were always forming different faces, depending on the light, or what I was feeling that day, and so our days passed somehow, under the watchful eyes of our lost families, happy, angry, sad, swinging in the wind above the windows.

One day when Kato Sensei was not there, a sudden gust of wind blew our *teru-teru-bozu* dolls right off their moorings, and the whole string of them went flapping and flying through the classroom like a dragon.

Hurry, Miss Yamada said. Catch them before they hit the floor.

Koichi was the first to react and he leaped from his crate chair, tearing through the room and causing a great commotion. With a flourish, he took the tail of the dragon and shook it up and down excitedly, and before anyone could stop him he went dashing through the room and over to the corner where all the *hibakusha* sat. They grabbed at the dragon's tail and he got them all up chasing after it, and soon even Miss Yamada took hold of the *teru-teru-bozu* string, and we all went dancing and frolicking around the room flaring and snorting like dragons.

Finally, though, the wind blew so hard that a piece of wood broke off a window frame and hit one of the younger boys in the shoulder, cutting him slightly, and he wailed and raised such a stir that the next day a man came and screwed tin sheets over the empty window frames. That kept things in place, but it made the room awfully dark, and when the wind blew off the sea and rolled up the Motoyasu, those tin sheets rattled and thundered so loudly we could not hear our teachers' voices.

Those were the times when not even Yamada Sensei's gentle hand could calm the class. Only the firm hand of Kato Sensei kept some semblance of order.

Flag Lunch

Sometimes my aunt prepared a Japanese-flag lunch for me— *onigiri,* a triangle of white rice or barley with a red pickled plum in the middle. The pits of these plums were so sour and salty that I used to take them out and give them to Koichi, who loved to suck them as if they were candy.

Many of my classmates were poorer than poor. They didn't have much rice and lived mostly on sweet potatoes and Japanese yams. Apart from the nutritional defects of such a diet, the olfactory effects were quite remarkable. Many a lesson was disrupted by the sound of breaking wind and the great hilarity this caused among the boys. Once when I'd had nothing but sweet potatoes to eat for several days, I felt one coming on and I tried to rush out of the room. But it was too late. I only got as far as the doorway when some *onara* gas exploded out of me.

Uh-oh, Hana-ko, one of the boys cried out. You ate sweet potatoes again.

I was so embarrassed that I answered him without thinking. No, I didn't. It was kabocha squash.

This seemed even funnier and the whole class started laughing.
Kabocha squash is very healthy, I protested.

Well, it doesn't smell very healthy, one of the older boys,
Nagata, stated for all the world to hear.

That will be enough, Yamada Sensei said in her firmest voice,
saving me even further embarrassment. I'm having kabocha
squash for lunch today, and I will not have you ruin it for me.

That quieted him and we went back to our lessons, but for a
long time after that, whenever a boy wanted to tease me, he called
out: kabocha squash!

Following that incident, I used to watch what Yamada Sensei
was eating for lunch, for her family had connections and was
rather better off than most of us. They had one of the new barracks
houses the Americans had built, and she could have eaten white
rice any time she wanted. But usually it was just potatoes or
kabocha squash or simply a few pickles and warm tea.

Late in the year, when the sun rose so late that it never seemed
to peek above our window before afternoon, I was awakened early
by the sound of my aunt heading off for work. We called it a
window, because it comforted us to call it that, but it was more
like an empty space she had left for the stove to vent, an oval
between the odd slats of wood and tin sheets she had tacked to
the walls in an attempt to keep the winter out. It may have been
cramped, but at least no one called it the Blue Sky Club.

From the doorway, as she opened it, I caught a glimpse of a sky
of pink and orange. Quickly, I rose and went outside to marvel at
the glory of the sunrise. How pleasing for the eye to look beyond
the broken city—its drab, determined streets, for poverty is always
brown and grey—and fly to where the mountains loomed, severe,
austere, but resplendent green in the places where the pine trees
grew. A silver sliver of a moon was setting in the western sky,
dozing off to sleep. The sun, the moon, two heavenly bodies in
one sky: it was an auspicious sign. I skipped off to school, singing
all the way. For I had *onigiri* to eat for lunch that day.

Suddenly, there came upon me the unmistakable odor of
steaming rice. The smell was so rich and appealing—it was white

rice for sure—that I started to follow it. I wouldn't go far, I told myself, and besides, wasn't I always early for school? But after a couple of turns down unfamiliar paths, I found myself in a confusing jumble of shanties and barracks houses. And then I saw the sign on the stone gate. This was where my father had worked, back when our family was still a family, before the bomb and the *yurai* ghosts and all the *teru-teru-bozu* dolls.

But we live in the present when we are young and I put those thoughts away to follow the wondrous scent. It seemed to tease me on, riding the east wind's back, leading me to a cluster of mean shacks that had sprung up along the edges of the army base, flimsy structures of wood and corrugated metal and anything else that would serve the purpose.

At least they provided some kind of shelter. Many people did not even have that much. There were whole families living on the streets, while others huddled in the shadows of the huts, as if hoping to derive some warmth from them, some sense of place where they'd feel safe.

Who could be steaming white rice here, I wondered, in these surroundings? And then I found the house. There was a big American army Jeep parked in front, and yet it hardly looked better than the other huts. I was pondering this when two men, GIs, came galumphing out the door with their big boots on. They looked at me and one of them went to say something, but the other one stopped him and then they hopped in their Jeep and sped off into the morning.

I should not have felt the slightest bit of envy for the people of that hut, for I had two barley *onigiri* with me for my lunch. These were the first ones I'd ever made. The shape was not good, but they held together, and the smell of the barley and the plum lingered on my fingers.

Yet this was white rice they were cooking, and it had been so long since I'd eaten my fill of it that I lost my manners completely and trotted around the hut to see the steaming pot for myself. There was no woman in the courtyard—that surprised me—only a homeless boy, older than me and stronger, of course, but thin and poorly clothed.

I knew I had gone too far when I went behind the house, and now there was something about this boy that frightened me. Might he hurt me? Should I report him to the owners of the house? He has an uneasy look and his eyes are not steady and when he straightens up I can see he's almost as tall as a man. He looks at me strangely, and when he opens his mouth to speak, I see it is full of broken teeth and I become so frightened that I run for the schoolyard as fast as I have ever run.

It's only when I get to the bridge that I finally slow down. I see a policeman at the crossroads and wonder what I should do. Should I tell him about that boy? What if he steals that rice? The police would catch him. But what if they don't? Those people will lose their rice and their iron pot and that would cause them great hardship.

Once safe at school, I said nothing about my scare but made certain that everyone knew what I had for lunch. I announced to all my friends that I was going to have *onigiri,* that I'd made two for myself that morning, each with a pickled plum in it. And at lunch I made a terrible show of eating my *onigiri,* taking tiny bites, as tiny as any field mouse ever took, then pausing to savor them, to study the shape and texture of each barley triangle, and to marvel at the redness of the rising-sun plum. Then when I was sure the others had seen me, I nibbled another bit, only to pause again and savor it anew.

Only later did I think about that boy, that he must have been hungry, how much more so than I?

It was true that there were bad gangs—*yakuza*—all over Hiroshima. They'd set up faster than MacArthur in the shattered city. They used young kids, who were in great supply then, to steal for them, and in return the gangsters might give them food and clothes or a place to sleep at night.

We'd lost a rice pot that way, had it stolen one night out from under our noses. That was a tough few days, without a rice pot, but then we found it one morning with a note in it saying, Please forgive me. I'll repay you some day. But others had had it worse. There were all sorts of stories about these gangs and about the orphans, too, boys and even girls who'd escaped from the orphanages and gone around like wild creatures.

Still, that boy had been really hungry. What right had I to judge him? And here I'd been so worried that he'd steal my *onigiri* that I didn't even think to give him one.

Outside classes. (Courtesy of Honkawa Elementary School, Hiroshima)

CHAPTER FIVE

1947

Early in the new year, they gathered us all up and led us down to the courtyard. Principal Sensei has an important announcement to make, they told us. There's a very important visitor coming, an American.

A *gaijin?* What did he want? What did it mean? The boys were suspicious.

There's no need to worry, Yamada Sensei reassured us. He's a very nice man. He's come all the way from Tokyo to talk to us.

All the way from Tokyo? To talk to us? Why, Sensei?

Finally, they got us all assembled. A fine lot we made, too, haggard and ragged as they come. But we didn't know that, or rather we'd forgotten that we'd ever lived any other way, or if we remembered, we tried not to. And what did that life have to do with this one, anyway? I was with my friends, Midori and Kazuko. So closely did we sit together in the freezing classroom that Takahashi Sensei called us the Three Sisters.

Principal Sensei was a short man and he stood on his tiptoes when he introduced the important *gaijin.*

With the help of our friends from America, he began uncertainly, looking back at his visitor, whether out of respect or submission I could not tell, our Japanese nation has undertaken a number of important reforms.

From now on, he said, democracy—*minshu shugi*—must be the basis for our national life. The principles of democracy will guide our work and our preparations for the future. That is the will of our Emperor, that the Japanese people study democracy and embrace it in their daily lives.

This has a direct bearing on our school. Accordingly, I have been instructed by the prefecture of Hiroshima to begin instruction of democracy and democratic principles here in Honkawa Elementary School, immediately.

The American spoke next. There were some people from the newspapers there and they scrambled to write down what he said, even though he spoke in English and they had to translate it into Japanese.

His name was Dr. Howard Bell Sensei and he was the first American I'd ever seen who wasn't a GI. He was very tall and had kind eyes and not much hair and his speech was all about this new idea, demonkurasi. What did it mean, this word?

No one knew. Who could even pronounce it? But it was obviously important, because the Principal Sensei had called us all together in the cold to tell us about it.

I was a serious girl and so afterward, when we were back in class, I asked Yamada Sensei what demonkurasi was.

She paused and considered it a moment. It means the people, she said vaguely, something to do with people.

It comes from Greece, Mr. Kato said from his corner of the class.

Greece? Midori and I were even more baffled now and went to Akiko at lunchtime.

Oh, demonkurasi, she said. That comes from America.

Like cars? asked Midori. I have a picture of a Ford car, a brand-new one, and guess what? It's bright red.

A red car. We all thought that was too much and started giggling.

But why did Principal Sensei take us out in the cold and have this American come all the way from Tokyo?

I don't know, Akiko said. But did you see the way Mr. Kato was looking at Miss Yamada when we were walking? I think he likes her.

All day the demonkurasi matter puzzled me, and so finally I decided to risk her ire and raise it directly with my aunt. To my surprise, she took me seriously and looked me plainly in the eye.

Dr. Howard Bell, at Honkawa School, 1947. (Courtesy of Honkawa Elementary School, Hiroshima)

To begin with, the word is not demonkurasi but democracy, little one.

What is that? What does it mean?

It means that the country is supposed to work for the people, not the people work for the country.

That seemed clear enough and so I went to school the next day and told everyone that we didn't work for Japan anymore and that Japan had to work for us now. That seemed to amuse Miss Yamada but not Mr. Kato. He put an end to my foolishness with one stern look.

And then one day, it was Mr. Kato himself who gave us a lesson in this democracy. It was all about constitutions and principles of government and no one understood a word of it. But with Kato Sensei you did not ask questions.

Ping-Pong Boy

Aunt continued to support the two of us through her unstinting labor. She worked every day, it seemed, one time tearing apart fallen buildings, another carrying water pipes to reconnect the city's sewers. She even unloaded coal cars at the train yard for a while. Perhaps that hard labor explains part of it, how she lived and why she talked to herself in that odd high voice.

After eating dinner I would try to do my lessons. Often she would try to help. Soon enough I would see her eyes droop, then she'd recover, then drift off again, and so she became accustomed to falling asleep to the sound of my voice. Then I would have to be silent and have the whole long night to hide from the *yurai*— unless sweet sleep would come and save me.

My job was to work in the vegetable fields. Even before the season was on us, I was down at the garden plot we shared with our neighbors, setting my boundary stones and breaking the soil. It was hard work, even with the pick Aunt had purchased at the night market, and when I got home in the evening I was exhausted.

Our lives depend on that vegetable garden, my aunt told me, and she recited a whole litany of things that could doom us. You could get the seeds too wet in the winter or keep them too dry in the spring. A thousand other things threatened us too. Birds, they were the worst, and those sneaky raccoons, and there were weeds, weevils, chiggers, caterpillars, ants, dung beetles, snakes, mice and rats and rodents of every kind, grasshoppers, wasps, and locust swarms. Any of them could sneak up on you at any time.

They'll destroy the whole crop, she warned. They'll eat it all and then we'd both be beggars.

But worst of all, she warned me as forcefully as she could, were the gang boys. Take your eye off that pick, even for a minute, and it'll be gone before you know it. And then they'll come at night sometimes and steal everything you have, especially at harvest time. I was going to have to be very, very careful and work very, very hard.

About that time, Koichi moved into a small cramped hut not far from us, with his mother and two young brothers. They had spent much of the war in Tokyo. When the fire-bombing of Tokyo began in the spring of 1945, Koichi's family was evacuated to Hiroshima,* where they found temporary quarters near the Fukuromachi School, not far from the A-Bomb Zone. How they survived it no one knows. Some people called it a miracle. But now, Koichi's mother had the radiation sickness and sometimes my aunt would bring them food, and whenever I would talk with him and ask about his father, he would say, He's out in the Far Sea, fishing for tuna.

It took me a long time to understand what he meant by that.

In the meantime, I pickaxed and shoveled the ground and worked at our garden plot, watching for thieves, and in the dark of the new moon my aunt and I planted cabbages and daikon radish, and then, as the spring progressed, barley, squash, and sweet potatoes.

After his mother took sick, Koichi hardly ever came to school. Sometimes I would see him early in the mornings, leading his brothers through the streets and alleyways, looking for nails and cans and scraps of tin, and then after a while it was only his brothers who were doing that. Koichi was polishing boots near the base where the GIs lived.

Now here was something to talk about: the Americans. We surrounded him on the rare occasions when he managed to attend school and bombarded him with questions. What were they like, these GIs? Did they really eat steak with every meal?

Oh yes, Koichi assured us. They can have it for breakfast if they want. And they don't eat rice. They eat bread. That's why they're so big and strong.

And what about those Jeeps? the boys wanted to know. Had he ever been in one?

Sure, I have. All the time.

No, liar. What are they like? Are they fast?

Very fast. Three times I've driven with them around the city.

But aren't you afraid? Kazuko asked.

What's there to be afraid of?

That they'll steal you or maybe even kill you?

No, he said with a laugh, dismissing the absurdity with a wave of his hand. Americans are the friendliest people in the world.

That surprised us. The friendliest people in the world?

Then why did they do it? a voice called out. It was Nagata, the tallest boy in the class.

Yes, yes, we all thought. What had we done? Why had they dropped that evil bomb on us?

If Koichi didn't have an answer for something, he'd usually have a joke instead. But this time he just looked at Nagata and said:

I don't feel particularly dead today, do you? No, no, and no! We're alive! All of us—you, me, Akiko—we're alive. So let's be happy! We're the lucky ones.

And so he would go, talking and cracking jokes, always a smile on his face. He used to come to our house sometimes in the evening, after our dinner was over and the pots had been put away, and in the deep lingering twilight he would talk of things, and my aunt would reach for the rice pot, toss some in a bowl with a healthy scoop of vegetables, and hand it to him with some tea.

He'd made friends with some GIs, Tony and Joe, men whose boots he'd shined, and now he did errands for them and they'd taught him some English words and how to play Ping-Pong.

Even today, I remember some words he taught me: Hey, Joe, shine ur chews? One pinny.

Koichi had a dream. Forget about being a fisherman; he would go to America. His friends would take him there. He'd be a carmaker, go to Detroit. Why not? Already he could draw cars—Jeeps, trucks, and sports cars. And after that he'd take everything he'd learned and bring it all back here, to Japan, and we'd make big cars too. Why not?

All over the city the ground had been broken for gardens that spring. Half the Honkawa School yard had been dug up and planted in sweet potatoes. It was the job of Akiko's class to plant and guard those fields.

All those sweet potatoes, I teased her. They're as bad as kabocha squash. Why couldn't you plant some spinach or cabbage? Anything but sweet potatoes.

But those were the only seeds we could get, she objected.

Can't the birds or the butterflies bring you something? came a familiar joking voice from behind the stone pile.

It was Koichi. Where have you been? we all asked.

Oh, here and there, he said blithely.

What are you doing here? Kato Sensei has been looking for you.

I just happened to be strolling through the area, he said casually. So I thought I'd come by and see about my sweet potatoes. I'd like mine roasted, please, with some pineapple on the side.

Pineapple indeed. When did he ever have pineapple?

Oh, just yesterday, he assured us, and he swore it was true.

But how could this be?

The Americans, of course. They had pineapple, and they had oranges, too, cans and cans of them. He'd seen them, right there at the ABCC.*

The ABCC? What is that? But before we could find out, he turned and ran off.

Oranges and pineapple? we wondered. Maybe we should go to the ABCC, too. But my aunt would have none of it.

I don't care what kind of fruit they have, she said. They're not going to get their hands on you. Not as long as I have any breath in me.

So another mystery was added to my life, the Atomic Bomb Casualty Commission. Just what went on in that building on the hill that everyone was so afraid of, everyone but Koichi?

I usually went to our garden plot directly after school. Happily, my path took me past a kindergarten. That was always something to look forward to as I headed off to my work: the sound of the children, laughing, playing, shouting. One time, I still remember, there were three of them, lying on their backs in the bright sunlight, burbling and singing to the open sky:

Oh, we are the children of the cloud.
Do not tell us who we are. We will tell you; we see far.
Over mountain, over sea, rising as high as you can see.
We are the children of the cloud.

Their voices sounded so sweet that I couldn't help but stop and listen. But still, when I saw clouds, they always reminded me of food and how hungry I always was.

Across the street from the Honkawa School was an empty field. There were some white cosmos flowers in it and yellow blossoms growing among the weeds. Shepherd's-purse grass had come back again.

Somehow the rumor had arisen that Koichi was popular with the Americans—so popular that he rode around in a Jeep with his GI friends—because he was a spy. Why else would he spend so much time at that ABCC?

But my aunt would hear none of it. What could that boy be a spy about? she scoffed. Tin cans and shiny boots?

In any event, he never came back from his American friends without bringing us some candy or gum and a good story.

And then one day, he disappeared. We looked for them but the whole family was gone. His mother must have died, poor soul, my aunt concluded. And sure enough the next morning there was another *teru-teru-bozu* doll hanging on the dragon string above the windows. It was Kazuko who saw it first. But Koichi was nowhere to be found.

A couple of months passed. My aunt had built a new wall for our barracks house, with places for two windows and a door. The neighbors helped, and just before summer vacation came, we got word that our ration of window glass would be delivered soon. Windows! At last we could keep the mosquitoes out. But it was not to be. The glass was stolen before we had a chance to install it. My aunt took the loss without a word and nailed the old boards back in place. But for three nights she stayed awake in case the thieves returned.

On the third night, we heard a strange noise outside. My aunt took a pot to bang on in one hand and a broom in the other and went outside, only to find him there.

Stop, Mrs. Takeda! Don't you recognize me?

Koichi? Whatever are you doing out at this time of night? Come into the house, child, and let me see you.

Poor Koichi. He looked very thin. He was trembling and his feet were all chapped and red. In fact, he looked like a beggar.

Warm as it was outside, Aunt went and put her cotton overcoat on him, but he kept trembling.

Tell me what happened, she said. We thought you had gone to the Orphans' Evacuation Center.

He didn't answer. He just stood there in the middle of the tiny room with the cotton coat on him, trembling.

Are you hungry? my aunt asked and went directly and poured him a bowl of potato dumpling soup without waiting for an answer. He drank it greedily and then another. He must not have eaten in many days. Finally, he recovered a bit and began to tell us his story.

When my mother died, they came and took me to the War Orphans' Evacuation Center in Hiroshima City, he said, me and my two brothers. But they wouldn't let me come back to Honkawa School or visit my GI friends. How am I supposed to make money? I asked them. But they didn't seem to care. The asylum had rules.

They moved him again, this time to a center on Ninoshima Island. That was even worse. They were very strict; there was a rule for and against everything. They shaved his head and washed him in caustic lye and scrubbed him until his skin turned red.

Wanted to make sure they killed the fleas, my aunt said.

Well, from that day until now, he continued sadly, I never had a moment to myself. School in the morning, then exercise and donkey's work. Carrying stones, digging fields, and the worst: the salt flats.

But even here he made a joke and claimed that his best friend there was a lamb. Yes, he insisted, that lamb went everywhere with me.

And when he told them that he had a right to stay in the city and earn his own living—these were his democratic rights—they said, You have no parents, and no relatives have come for you. There are too many children in the city as it is.

Then they sent him to another orphanage, in the mountains. The people in the village there were mean. I understood, he said. They were poor. There was hardly anything to eat, and what am I but just another mouth to feed?

So how did you get here? my aunt asked.

I ran away. I had to.

When?

Two days ago.

Why don't you tell us what happened?

Well, he replied slowly, it was like this. About a week ago, I was working in the fields when I saw another kid steal some potatoes. I tried to tell him to stop, but he ran away. I followed him to the neighbor's farm and at that moment the farmer came up and accused me of being a thief. I tried to explain it to him, but he wouldn't listen. He took me back to the orphanage, and they told me I had to make an apology, a *dogeza,** to the villagers. But I hadn't done anything wrong and I wouldn't do it. After that they said I was just a troublemaker and they wouldn't let me play Ping-Pong anymore. That was the only thing I liked about the place.

And now you're back here, my aunt said.

An Imaginary Sword

Koichi stayed with us for several days, but he didn't dare return to school. The truant officer would be looking for him and they'd send him back to the orphans' asylum if they caught him.

Why don't they leave me alone? he pleaded. I was fine here. I worked; my brothers collected cans; we had enough to eat. If I could only go back to my corner, I could shine shoes again.

But they'll catch you, my aunt said. You know that. You're only twelve years old.

It's not the truant officer I'm worried about, he said after a moment's pause. It's my location, my corner—they've taken it away from me. The yakuza control it now. It's so close to the American base. I'll never get it back unless I fight them all.

And with that he drew an imaginary samurai sword and waved it with mock menace, setting us all to laughing despite ourselves.

And what about your brothers? my aunt asked.

They were adopted by some farmers, he said sadly. But I don't need to be adopted. If I could work . . . I was making good money. Tony and Joe were always going places with me. They took me all over. I rode in a Jeep a hundred times. I helped them find things; I could talk to them, show them how to get around, be useful. I had money then, good American greenbacks.

Tony and Joe, they're my friends. I'll find them again. I have my shoeshine kit. I'll find another place. I'll say, Hello, Mister. Shine ur chews? Hello, GI. Where's ur sister? See? I can take care of myself. I can do that. I can take care of myself and my brothers, too.

You could stay here, my aunt said after a while. We could make space for you. And so he stayed with us. He didn't have any money to pay for his supper, but he sure kept us laughing with his jokes.

But then one day he was not there when I came home from gardening, and for days no one knew what had happened to him. Later, Akiko, who was about his age, told me she'd heard that the police had found him down by the GI base and they had taken him back to the orphanage on Ninoshima Island.

Koichi. (Drawing by Yoshiko Jaeggi, courtesy of Shizumi Shigeto Manale)

We never saw him after that. But later I heard that he'd learned to play Ping-Pong so well that he'd become a champion and that he'd been at a tournament where there were GIs playing and he'd beaten some of them and after that they'd adopted him and taken him back to America.

I wondered. Did his dream come true? Did he ever make it to Detroit? For months whenever I saw an airplane, I would imagine that Koichi was in it, waving from his window seat, as he flew off to a new life in America.

Sweet-Potato Fields and Cotton-Candy Clouds

Sometimes, when it was Akiko's turn to take the after-school shift in the sweet-potato fields, I'd tag along with her.

Hey! I brought a guest today, she said the first time, introducing me to her sixth-grade friends. I knew most of them from our time in the single classroom, but to be friends with them outside of school, that was another matter. At first I was nervous. They were sixth-graders and the bloom of life was beginning to make them frisky, none more so than Akiko.

I'd brought my own shovel, its tip bright from constant contact with the soil. She's too little to work in our field, some dumb boy said in a bossy voice. She'll mess things up.

But Akiko defended me. Don't worry, she said, with a flip of her long black hair. She's my friend. She can pull weeds with me. And you can go back to doing what you do best—chasing grasshoppers.

Ooooh. Her friends were impressed. How easily she had made that boy look foolish.

After about an hour, a samurai war broke out among the boys. Akiko and I had finished weeding our rows and we walked across the road and lay down by a little patch of white cosmos flowers where the ground was soft. The other girls followed us. There must have been ten of them. A slight breeze was coming off the sea, full of sun and the promise of the season, and with it the contentment that came from being with Akiko.

From where we lay, the sky reached high above us and the mountains seemed soft and green. Far away, an old coal bus crept up the steep, sandy road heading to Hon-chii. I put my head on Akiko's lap and drifted off to sleep.

Fight! Fight! Fight! Across the way the war raged. One by one the boys who'd been defeated came over to join us, dejected but not surprised.

I feel even hungrier when I run, the one with no front teeth said.

It's not fair, his bald-headed friend replied. They had lunch today.

Look at that cloud, the first one said. Doesn't it look like white rice balls?

And there, a red-cheeked casualty of the war games added. Doesn't that cloud look like omelet-rice?

I see a big koi fish, Akiko said, her voice both gentle and mocking. Can you see it? It looks like Nagata, she said with a laugh, and her friends laughed with her. He was the boy she liked, who at that moment was across the street slaying his mock enemies.

Koi carp? Another girl took up the thought. Yummmm! If I could only have my grandmother's koi carp and seaweed again.

*Kibi-dango** dumplings, one of the girls said with great longing.

No, no, no, the bald-headed boy objected. *Okonomiyaki** pancakes.

*Kinako mochi,** his red-cheeked friend retorted, sticky rice cake covered with soybean powder and sugar.

Kinako mochi, kinako mochi, kinako mochi, the girls began to sing.

Stop talking about food, the boy with no front teeth said with a laugh. It just makes me hungrier.

We eat with our eyes, don't we, girls? Akiko laughed and the sound of her girlish laughter carried across the street and caught Nagata's ear this time. He put down his warrior's guard and sauntered over.

What is this singing for? he asked with a shy smile. Shouldn't you be working?

Not me, Akiko replied gaily. We are the girls of Honkawa School and we eat with our eyes. The clouds are cotton candy—and you are the prize.

And with that, she jumped up and started to chase him down the road, with all ten of the girls and me behind her, yelling, Koi carp. Catch that koi carp, now.

Mysterious River

In the long summer evenings, we sometimes went down to the Motoyasu to sit on the banks beside the cool, swirling water. I was still afraid of the river; the thought of the spirits of everyone who died there terrified me. But if I went with Akiko and her friends, then I didn't worry. I knew I'd be all right.

Life was beginning to return to the estuary. Reeds were growing in clumps, and here and there a few fingerlings worked against the steady current. And there, on the sandy bottom, might be a turtle poking for some food.

People had begun to fish in the river again, even though the mayor had put up signs all along the bridges warning people not to eat anything they caught there.

Look, ghosts, Akiko said suddenly one evening, pointing at the swaying reeds, for she knew how much I was afraid of them.

No, they're not, I answered, hoping to end the discussion there. But Akiko had mischief in mind.

Yes, she said. Those are ghosts, ghosts of all the people who died in the river. Look, Hanako, they are beckoning to you: come with us to the dark waters.

Standing by the fire he had built to cook the fish he never caught, Nagata snickered. If it was ghost stories Akiko wanted to tell, he could do better than that.

I am the ghost of Octopus Bonze, he said in a deep, scary voice. Listen to my tale of woe-oh-oh-oh-oh. Ohhh, it was a dark and lonely night. Bats were circling everywhere, looking for blood to drink. Evil spirits were all about. High in the sky a pale green moon cast pale green shadows across the land along the river. All was still. Only the owl was calling to her mate. Hoo-hoo-hoot! Then a young man came walking along the banks of the river. It was the young *ainoko ni sei,** GI Jack. He was tall and thin, and he had one round eye and the other one was slanted. His mother was American and his father Japanese, and when he spoke Japanese it came out of the right side of his mouth. But when he spoke English, it came out of the left.

I remember him, Akiko interrupted. He looks like that silly boy, Nagata.

Silence, female, or I will turn you into a sea serpent, Octopus Bonze thundered, and he flopped around with his eight long tentacles, tickling the little ones. Then he continued his tale.

Suddenly, GI Jack heard an unusual sound. What is this? It sounds like a lady crying. Yes! A beautiful lady. What has happened to you, beautiful lady?

I have lost my son to the river, she said in her sweet, sweet voice. I've been searching for him everywhere. Won't you come help me, here by the water's edge?

Don't go, GI Jack, the wise owl warned. Don't go down to the banks of the Motoyasu.

But all he could hear was the sound of the water splashing against the rocks.

Here, GI Jack, just a little farther.

No, no, the she-owl screeched, don't go down by the riverside, not on this night when the moon is green.

But GI Jack did not heed her. He hurried through the tall grass. Thorns cut his feet, but still he followed the lady's voice.

Come, my friend GI Jack, come a little closer. It's my son; I've lost him. I've lost him in the waters.

And on GI Jack went, through the thick grass toward the swirling water. He looked for her everywhere, but all he heard was the sound of splashing water. Suddenly, the noise grew so loud that it burst his ears. Yes! The stars were falling in the river.

She must be a *kappa,* I whispered, picturing an ugly eight-armed water monster.

No! It was the spirits of the people that drowned in the water, begging GI Jack to help them.

Nagata had us in his hands now, and he held us there for a long time in perfect silence before he spoke again.

So many stars fell that a great tsunami rose up. GI Jack ran and ran. But nobody can outrun a tsunami. It swept over him in a second and broke him in half. The Japanese half was saved. But the American half was swept away, never to be seen again.

And then what happened? Akiko finally asked.

We all leaned close to him to hear. And suddenly he screamed: *Ahhhg!* I am Octopus Bonze!

And we all jumped out of our skins and into the stars.

Look, he said after a long while, there's Orion. Can you see? He's got a bamboo sword, hanging from his sash.

Why can't it be a fish instead of a sword? I asked.

They all laughed and called me a silly raccoon, and then for a long time everything was silent. I lay close to Akiko and watched the fire burn down, and later that night, when the flames were almost out, I heard a fish jump. It must have been a big one, because when it smacked the water, it sounded like a tree branch snapping. Slowly, slowly, life was returning to the river.

CHAPTER SIX

New White Shoes

The first day back at school that fall, Akiko showed up wearing a pair of spanking-new white sports shoes. Akiko, the one whose clothes were always grey and patched together, with new shoes? We were flabbergasted. Within three minutes the whole school was talking.

White sports shoes, the older girls whispered. Did you hear? Akiko's got new shoes. They're beautiful. Magic, another one said.

No one had ever seen anything like them, the way the white gleamed in the sunlight. Even Midori was impressed. We all gathered around Akiko, talking excitedly, just as she must have wanted.

Here, let me look.

No!

You've been there long enough. It's my turn now; let me have a chance.

Finally, the commotion grew so loud that Nagata rose from his orange-crate chair and, abandoning his customary air of indifference, wandered over to see what the fuss was all about.

White shoes, he said simply, then turned and walked away.

But the rest of us were intensely curious. Where on earth did you get them? We pressed around her, waiting for her answer.

Oh, she said casually, they're just a little gift I got.

From whom? Who could afford such luxury?

But Akiko refused to tell. That's my little secret, she said coyly. For days, that was all anyone could talk about, just as she must have wanted. Where could they have come from? Who could have given a gift like that? And if, by chance, the discussion in the schoolyard turned to anything else, she found a way to revive it.

Can you watch my white sports shoes, Hana-chan? she'd ask. I don't want to spoil them running in the courtyard. Or, could you keep my white sports shoes for a while? I have an important test to take.

She even found ways to bring the subject up when it had nothing to do with anything, such as the story she concocted about going to the night market to buy a box to put her white sports shoes in at night. As if the shoes needed a bed of their own to sleep in.

Despite the leg injury she suffered in the earthquake bomb, Akiko was the fastest girl in Honkawa School. She could beat all but a handful of the boys. We were counting on her for Field Day, for Principal Sensei had decided to start the races up again in October. It was an old tradition at our school. The boys, of course, had already formed their teams. Kato Sensei was going to train them.

We girls were left on our own, but not for long. Without a word, Akiko came to school one day without her dazzling white sports shoes, for they were indeed two sizes too big for her and she'd had to put cotton in them to keep them on her feet. At recess that morning, she walked out into the schoolyard in her bare feet and ran two tours around the sweet-potato fields, and in the afternoon she ran the circuit three more times.

The next morning at recess I took off my *geta* sandals, and Akiko and I ran barefoot around the courtyard, out beyond the school grounds, and past the patch of cosmos flowers, their yellow hearts a touch of gold in the bright sunlight. Out past the stone piles we went, over paths we'd beaten going to our gardens. We girls had a team of our own now, and soon my friends Midori and Kazuko were on it.

Three Eggs

Midori is a special case because she is my good friend and I know she will read this, so I need to choose my words carefully.

Of all my friends, she was the only one who still had her mother and father. This made for complicated feelings on my part. I longed for my own parents constantly and just to have life the way it was, even if it meant that my mother had to be in the mountains all the time. At least I would have her. But it would not, could not be.

Of course, Midori could not understand at first. Her own life had been dramatic enough just getting through the war. But now her father was vice principal at the high school, and they were living in one of those double barracks houses that General MacArthur had built. The whole family was together. Midori had pretty clothes all the time, it seemed, and bright-colored ribbons. Of course I resented her at first.

She seemed to recognize this early on and would accommodate my moods. She was a cheerful girl and extremely clever. Whenever I didn't understand something, it was she who would explain it to me. She seemed to enjoy that. It was Midori too who finally explained to me what democracy meant: no more war. That's what her father told her.

That was good enough for me. Ask the people who have lived through one war if they want another.

What struck me the first time I visited her home was the smell of new-sawn wood. They had two rooms, a dining room with a small kitchen and a bedroom, and, better yet, a wild mouse in a birdcage. Her mother was very gracious and offered me some tea and a rice cookie. I had been worried she would hate me for having been so rude to her at school, but now I grew comfortable there and happy.

Midori had a lot of books at home. I loved it when she would ask her mother if she could take one out and show it to me.

Of course, she would say. Just be careful, dear. Those books are very rare.

Indeed they were. Toward the end of the war, Midori had been evacuated from the city, and with two crates of books and a few belongings she had walked to a refuge her mother had found on the other side of Mount Shinaki. There she'd stored the books in a

Shinto shrine, for many of them were very old and had been with her family for generations. And when the war was finally over and their barracks house was built, she brought them down to Hiroshima.

Compared to the way I lived with my aunt, Midori's life was paradise. One morning during recess, as we were practicing for Field Day, I finally asked her: Midori-chan, doesn't your mother ever get angry? Doesn't she ever yell at you?

I remember one time when she lost her temper and got really, really mad at me, she said sadly. I felt so ashamed of myself.

A good Nightingale lets the other person talk. We were running and coming to the cosmos flower field. For a while there would be no one who could overhear us. Akiko was far ahead of us, her bare feet flying. Already the boys working the sweet-potato fields had stopped jeering her and just shook their heads as she ran by.

Hana-chan, this is my secret, so please don't tell anyone, Midori said.

I promised and we made the *yubi-kiri-genman** sign.

It happened last year, when things were so bad. You remember?

Yes.

Somehow my mom had managed to find three eggs. Three big eggs: can you imagine? I was so excited to see them that I had an accident. I wanted to show them to my grandmother, you see? But they fell on the floor. I don't know how it happened. I . . . I didn't mean to be so clumsy.

There were tears in Midori's eyes, and I could see she was about to cry. So, just to prove how clumsy people can be, I pretended to trip. I fell on her, and we both tumbled to the ground laughing, laughing.

And what did you do? I asked, as I seized her in a sumo hug. Quick as a cat, she broke free.

Oh, I scraped them up off the floor and put them in a cup, she said. Mom was so mad she made tiger eyes at me. Oh, she was angry; I've never seen her like that. I was lucky Grandmother was there, but still, my mother refused to speak to me for several days.

And with that, she scampered off, and it was all I could do to catch her.

Teachers' Night Duty

In those days, one of the teachers would stay on after school to stand night duty and keep an eye on the premises. We children could stay with them if we needed to. Occasionally, we'd go home after school but come back in the evenings, just to be with the teacher for an hour or two, especially if it was Mr. Kato.

He was the strictest of all the teachers and he had a short temper. But on those evenings, he was more relaxed, and when he was really at ease, he liked to sing navy songs and talk about the way things used to be in Hiroshima, our city on the river by the sea.

But it was the way he talked about the stars and planets that intrigued me. One day, he announced in class that Jupiter would be visible in the eastern sky that night, just after the sun went down. I harassed my aunt until she walked me to the school and left me there, along with Kazuko and Midori.

Kato Sensei had a navy telescope. If there was a special occasion, he would always bring it, and that night, if the sky was clear, we were going to look at Jupiter and her baby moons.

Ah, the Three Sisters, Kato Sensei said when he saw Kazuko, Midori, and me. He bowed to my aunt respectfully. Welcome to our school.

Then all the girls rushed around him to see the telescope, bowing and greeting him with a chorus of: Good evening, Kato Sensei. Thank you so much for inviting us to stay at school. We are so glad you accepted our request.

The boys stayed off at a safer distance, for Kato Sensei had been known to slap them if they said something rude or disrespectful. They took their caps off and bowed to him, saying, *Onegai shimasu,* please accept us, in voices so loud and raucous that they frightened the crows away.

Mr. Kato scolded them for that, and he instructed Nagata, whose voice could be heard above the others calling out the greeting, to come close to him.

I don't want to hit you this time, Kato Sensei said calmly. I just want you to understand. Discipline and respect. The future of our Japan is in your hands.

In Nagata's hands? Akiko whispered, loudly enough for everyone to hear. Can you imagine that? Octopus Bonze? Our future's in his hands?

Even Mr. Kato had to smile at that one.

We went up the staircase very carefully to the roof of the school, for here and there a step was missing. From up there we had a view over all the city. In one direction lay the mountains, rising sharp and green above the busy, battered streets. And in the other lay the river, the harbor, and then open water as far as the Inland Sea.

We looked at the stars when the sun went down. I was with Kazuko.

Is it true? she asked. Do people really turn into stars after they die? Because I want to know which ones my parents are.

That one's my mother, I replied, pointing to the brightest star of all, eager to claim it for my own.

And later, when I'd looked at Jupiter through Kato Sensei's telescope and seen the tiny moons snuggling so near to it, I thought of my mother, and the moons were the three of us, Makiko, Tadashi, and me.

You are so lucky, Hanako, having an aunt to take care of you, Kazuko said to me. I have no family left. I'm a *hibakusha*.

No, you're not, I insisted. There's nothing wrong with you.

Yes, there is, she said. I might have to go to an orphanage soon.

But what about your cousin? That's your home. You can always stay there, can't you?

I don't know, she finally said. Maybe I can't. There is a man who has asked her to marry him. But he doesn't want me. That's what he told her: no *hibakusha*. Why did we have to have that war, Hana-chan? Why did we have to have that stupid war?

Baby Cranes

At the top of this universe of ours, the one that holds the earth and sky up, there is a hole, and through this hole, if you know where to look, you can enter another universe, far away from this one of our own.

Viewed from that upper universe, our earth is just a tiny dot, a star floating in the sea, and our Japan is just a dot on that dot, a speck on a speck in this lower universe.

Up on the roof, Kato Sensei was warming up to tell another one of his stories.

A long, long time ago, he began, before the Edo time,* a young woodcutter was traveling through Hokkaido. It was very cold, and the winter snow was falling on the frozen reeds and rushes. From the forest, he heard the call of the baby cranes. They are hungry. They're calling for their mother, who has gone to look for food. But that was hours and hours ago and she has not returned. The baby cranes are calling, calling for her.

The story droned on, and I fell into a kind of trance. Suddenly my mother appeared before me in great vividness. We are at home, and I am sitting close beside her. She has a book in her hand, and for one second, one speck of time, I believe again.

To hide my pain and confusion, there on the roof, I rise on one leg and slowly arch my back. I spread my graceful, flightless wings, bend my long, white neck beneath one wing, and sleep. But we are hungry cranes, faint from lack of food and water. Where is our mother? I crane my neck; I scan the winter skies. And then I hear the hunter's gun. I gasp; I twist; I twitter. And then to the great amusement of my class, if not Kato Sensei, I tumble to the floor and die.

A crane is much smarter than you are, one of the *hibakusha* boys teases me when I get up.

And a crane will live longer than you will, I snap back at him.

What a terrible, thoughtless thing to say. I am ashamed and stay away from the boy and Kato Sensei for a long time that night. But later, when he is singing one of his navy songs, I creep up close to him, and he touches me oh-so-lightly on the head. Then, when we are going home, he catches my eye and holds it, and I bow my respects and apology to him, and after that I make more effort to be respectful.

As for the poor *hibakusha* boy, we paid our last respects to him a few months later. It still haunts me that I never apologized to him, and now that I long to do so, I cannot.

Undo-kai

As Field Day—*Undo-kai*—approached, Akiko stopped wearing any shoes at all to school. See? she asked me one day. Touch the bottoms of my feet: they're as hard as brick. Nobody is going to beat me.

And when we ran that morning, we saw a new patch of white petals blooming in the fields beyond the schoolyard: cosmos flowers. Akiko stopped and picked one as she ran by and held it in her hand, and we did the same, Midori, Kazuko, and me, and together we ran like the wind.

Bit by bit, *Undo-kai* caught the imagination of the Honkawa School. A week before the grand event, our teachers cut their lessons short, and we practiced *tama-wari.** Over and over, Mr. Kato took us through our paces, showing us the best way to throw the red and white balls, like a man, without letting your arm flop around.

Every morning at recess, we ran three turns around the school grounds, two teams of boys and we girls behind Akiko. We ran four more turns instead of eating lunch because we couldn't afford to run after school. It would be harvest soon and we had to be at our fields the minute class let out, for there were thieves about and hungry, hungry bugs, and every potato and individual squash was important.

The woman next door, a friend of my aunt's, had made me a pair of *wara-zori* sandals from braided strands of rice straw, as my old *geta* clogs were missing their straps and hardly worthy of the name anymore. It was very kind of her. But secretly, I'd been longing for some white sports shoes, like the ones Akiko wore.

My aunt must have noticed my disappointment and tried to persuade me to wear the new sandals. In the old days, she said, we used to wear *wara-zori* and walk for miles in them. We even ran.

I said nothing.

I don't want you to forget the kindness my friend has showed you, Hana-chan. You will honor her by wearing your pretty *wara-zori* on *Undo-kai*. Run fast and win a prize.

But how can I run fast wearing *wara-zori?* I asked.

These are not an ordinary pair, my aunt retorted. Look at all the work in them, how beautiful they are, all pretty and new. Here, try them on.

It was true; they were soft and comfortable. I was able to run and jump a bit in them. But still, we were the barefoot girls; that's what Akiko called us. No one was going to slow us down with silly *wara-zori* sandals.

But my aunt could not understand. If only things were the way they were before, she said sadly. I could have easily bought you running shoes. But no. They had to have their war.

Nothing I could do or say could change her mind. Finally, I went and told Akiko about it and together we hatched a plan.

Field Day came at last. Carefully and with a great show of devotion, I put on my new *wara-zori* and walked to school. Akiko was already there, wearing her dazzling sports shoes. Midori had a new pair of sports shoes, too, and although they were not so audacious as to be white—her parents did not want to be that ostentatious—they actually fit her, which was an advantage because she was the slowest one of us.

Kazuko was fast and her feet were almost as fleet as Akiko's, but she had nothing but her sister's *geta* to wear on *Undo-kai*, and they were so old that she could hardly walk in them. Still, she wore them proudly.

Shizuko was Miss Yamada's niece. She was faster than Midori and always had a smile on her face when she ran. Today, for *Undo-kai*, she was wearing her aunt's old ballet slippers and a look of unusual determination.

Everyone saw what everyone wore, but nobody said a word. But then I've noticed: it's the things people don't say that usually matter most.

The boys' teams had on their best shoes, too, and they eyed

us with their usual condescension. Principal Sensei must have noticed the sudden blooming of new footwear, and at the end of his speech, which was about how poor they were in Africa, he paused and looked at us and said something about shoes, and whether or not you had them or what kind they were, this was *Undo-kai*. It was a mark of the progress that the city and the school had made that we were having *Undo-kai* again. If the children of Africa, who never owned shoes or had enough food to eat and yet were able to run through the jungle all day, could do it, so ought we Japanese.

Of course, we were nervous. My aunt had managed to get time off from work that day, and I was glad that she was there to see me run. She had a parasol of sea-blue silk she'd found and cleaned, and she held it with a grace that belied her years of manual labor. Midori's father and mother were there and Akiko's cousins, and when Principal Sensei stopped talking he laid the prizes out on a table: little flags, lunchboxes, and two sets of *wara-zori* sandals with bright-red straps.

Finally, we walked up to the starting gate, each in our fine awkward shoes.

I watched Akiko closely, in her two-sizes-too-big running shoes. I tried to copy everything she did, for I had not told my aunt what we had plotted, and when we lined up to race, we took off our shoes and put them to one side with the proper grace, five pairs side by side. And off we set, the barefoot girls, with Akiko in the lead.

The boys, of course, were soon beyond us. Akiko picked up the pace and we followed her closely. Our feet knew the paths, and even Midori was running fast. As we were passing the slow boys' team, one of them tried to elbow Akiko, hoping to knock her off her stride. But she stepped lightly around him and picked up the pace.

We were working hard now, just to keep up. The first boys' team was still ahead of us. Out by the sweet-potato fields, they knocked a crate of rakes over and they spilled in our path—just by accident, of course—but Akiko saw them and motioned to us and we got over them easily. Then, as we neared the fields where the white cosmos flowers grew, Akiko passed into the lead, and for the first time all the boys were put in check.

One by one they challenged her and one by one they failed. Then, just as her victory seemed assured, she stopped. Was she hurt? Had she twisted an ankle or stepped on a thorn? We ran on even faster, and when we reached her, she handed us each a flower.

A few boys had run past us by then, and they looked at us with uncomprehending scorn. What were they doing, these foolish girls?

Once again, Akiko set about her task, running them down one by one, only this time they made way for her, and when she reached the last one, the boy with the red bandana, he gritted his teeth and willed himself to faster speed. She stayed on his heels until they approached the finish line, and then she passed him, a wide smile on her face.

Akiko had won and we five girls had beaten the slow boys badly. When we all arrived at the finish line, we cheered for ourselves and for our friends. Then we put on our shoes and went to our families, or what was left of them, and presented our flowers to each of them.

My aunt received hers with surprise.

It's a miracle, she said with a rare smile. I thought I'd never see flowers like this again. Thank you, my child, thank you.

Across the courtyard I saw Midori and her parents, their arms around each other, and oh how I wished my own mother were there. I could picture her so clearly, hugging me closely and saying, You are my miracle, Hana-chan. You are my cosmos flower.

Bananas

It was a cold, cold morning in early December, so cold that Miss Yamada had come to school early to light the stove. Ours was an old coal-burning beast they'd set on a slab of stone in the middle of the room so we could huddle around it—and not freeze to death, as Midori used to say.

Bit by bit the school was being repaired. We had some chairs now but still hardly any books. There was a kind of floor and doors on certain rooms, but the windows they promised still had not come.

It was only before class, under Miss Yamada's watchful eye, that something like democracy was allowed. We each took turns standing by the stove, while our friends counted to 100, and then our turn would end. It was not quite enough to warm you, but at least everybody got an equal chance.

As soon as class began, however, the law of equal chances gave way to the higher laws of force and celestial mechanics. The older kids claimed as their natural right the heat and vapors of Mercury, while we younger, weaker planets were cast out to the farther limits of our solar system, poor cold dependencies such as Uranus and Pluto. To cope with my cold and distant orbit, I usually wore an extra sweater and a vest so thick with cotton padding that my classmates called me *Daruma-san,* the fat little Buddha.

But even so, I caught a chill that day, and by the time I came home I had a fever and a badly swollen throat. It only got worse, and cozy as our little barracks house might be, nothing my aunt did could keep me warm. At night, as I lay there, it occurred to me that I might die. My mother was dead, and so were my father, sister, brother, grandmother, uncle, and two cousins. Didn't I deserve it too?

It was radiation sickness that scared me most. What was it that could kill people practically overnight? Why did some people die but not others? Because no one knew, no one talked about it.

I was very, very afraid that night. Then a strange thought came to me: I could see my mother if I died. At first that idea comforted me like a thick, warm blanket. But then, what if it weren't true? Was there really a Pure Land? Or was there only this land, the one that I could see? Back and forth these questions warred inside me, leaving me in great anxiety, lost between hope and fear. Finally, I slept, and in the darkness I heard my aunt singing in that curious private voice of hers.

Here, here, my little Hana-chan. I have bananas, sweet apples too. Eat these bananas. Eat, little one, eat this apple bun. Have your fill now and I'll go milk the goat and then we'll drink miso soup.

When I woke up, I was feeling better, and I found that there were indeed bananas and apples, glorious, glorious apples to eat. Many people in our neighborhood of barracks houses had pitched in to help, but no one had worked harder than the woman who had made my *wara-zori*. More than half the money for the apples had come from beneath her futon.

She came to see me the next morning with a long thin tube and a *mikan* orange. Your temperature is lower this morning, my flower, she said. Eat this and rest, and I'll come to see you again tomorrow with my friend, Mister Thermometer.

And she came back again with bananas and more apples. Apples. Just the sight of them cured me, I think, for within a few days I was up and ready to go back to school.

CHAPTER SEVEN

Rumors

During my sickness, a rumor had started up that I was a *hibakusha*. It wasn't true; I was in the mountains at Hon-chii, twenty kilometers away, when the A-Bomb hit. But people didn't really understand these things. Maybe twenty kilometers was not enough. And because no one knew, no one spoke about it. I could feel my friends pulling away from me, as if they might catch radiation disease if I touched them by mistake.

People thought you could pass it down to your children. Not just that it might be hereditary, but that touching someone could be enough to bring the sickness on. We'd seen what it did to people. I'd held my father's hand. Would it catch me too? I held my breath against the fear at night, and when the candle went out, I hid deep, deep beneath the blankets. If any part of me was exposed to the dark—a hand, the top of my head—I awoke with a start, and I would be terrified until I was safe again, buried deep beneath the covers.

Still, I was better off than most of them. I didn't have any burns; no harm had come to my arms or legs. And wasn't I part of the barefoot girls, the team that beat the boys?

Midori-chan was my best friend then, the only one I could talk to about what bothered me. Akiko had little interest in other people's troubles, not when there were boys around, and Aunt was hard to talk to. Midori persisted; that's what I liked about her. We grew closer when the others pulled back.

Don't worry, she assured me. You can't catch the radiation sickness and you can't give it to anyone. I know, because that's what my father says.

And how does he know?

He is Vice Principal Sensei and he knows all about MacArthur and our Japan.

I was not so sure, but one day by chance I met him at Midori's house.

It's simple, Hana-chan, he told me. Radioactivity cannot be contagious, nor does it have the least ability to transfer from one person's cells to another. It is not an infectious disease.

These words reassured me considerably, and I asked him many questions. But then, I always knew I'd be a nurse. After all, wasn't I little Nightingale-san?

One day on the way home from school one of the older girls, a rival of Akiko's for the boys' attentions, snuck up behind me and called me a strange little *hibakusha*. I ran home crying, and when my aunt found out, she went down to the school the next morning with her fists at the ready. And when the girl saw her coming, she quickly changed her tune and from then on she was nice to me.

I was hardly the only one who had been singled out like that. Finally, the teachers gathered all the healthy children together and for the first time, they tried to speak to us frankly about the Bomb. As a former naval officer, Kato Sensei was selected to speak first. It was not an easy matter to discuss, even without the *hibakusha* in the room.

The machine that destroyed our ancient city has brought us to this point, he said slowly, searching painfully for each word. That machine was born of science, but of a science driven mad by war.

But it seems to me that a new Japan is rising out of the ashes of the old, he continued. And that new Japan is you, our young heroes and cosmos flowers.

With that last unexpected allusion, he turned toward Akiko and bowed ever so slightly.

Each of you is a survivor of terrible things, he went on. It has been hard, very hard, for everyone.

But if the past makes us weep, we look forward to a better future. Each of you has defied enormous odds to be here—ten thousand to one. Do you know that? You are like lottery winners, ten-thousand-to-one lottery winners. And that is good, because our Japan, the new Japan, needs you badly now. So you must work very hard and you must have discipline.

Then Principal Sensei spoke up. This Honkawa Elementary School was one of the only structures standing after August sixth. Why were we so fortunate? Because our foundation was strong. The builders dug deep in the earth and made our walls thick and sound with brick, concrete, and steel.

So must our standards of education be dug deep into the earth and made strong with the brick and steel of books and pencils, pens, ink, and reference books.

We have made repeated requests for these materials to the Ministry in Hiroshima Prefecture and today, I am happy to announce that our appeal has been viewed with favor by the deputy mayor, the Honorable Shinzo Hamai.*

Then he paused and wiped his glasses, a sure sign that what he was about to say should be listened to.

It has come to my attention, he continued, glancing at me and several other children, that there are rumors going around this school concerning the effects of atomic radiation.

Scientists from Japan and the United States have been studying this matter very carefully. Some of you may have seen the ABCC Building not far from here. That's where the research, the collecting of information, takes place.

There is much we do not know about radiation disease. But there is one thing we do know. I can say it with great certainty: it is not contagious. Is a burned arm or broken leg contagious? No. Well, neither is radiation.

I will not tolerate rumors in this school that directly contradict these scientific facts. If your friend is suffering more than you, help him; don't turn your back. If your neighbors need your help, go and help them. Your school, your family, and your country, all are counting on you to do your duty.

And with that, he drew himself up to his full height and dismissed us with a stiff nod. Miss Yamada went and brought the *hibakusha* back, the ones they called the Rising Sun Class, and for a while his words did seem to help. Most of my wavering friends returned to me. But children can be nasty to each other, and the words that had been said to me, and the things that had been implied, gnawed away at my confidence and haunted me at night.

Pink Eraser

Someone was calling my name in the hallway. It was bald-headed Nagata, Octopus Bonze himself, the third member of his family to have the radiation disease, running toward me in great loping strides, his wooden *geta* clomping on the new floor and making a terrible noise.

Hey, you forgot your pencil, he said with a nervous grin when the clattering finally ceased.

That's not mine, I replied, looking with surprise at the pencil stub he was offering me.

Yes, it is. It's my New Year's gift for you, he whispered. I have new ones, you see, and he showed me two beautiful shiny pencils. One of them was bright yellow and it had a pink eraser on the end that had a clean, rubbery smell.

How did you get those? I asked.

Don't you know? I got them from one of the doctors at the ABCC Hospital. And with that, he galloped off toward his own uncertain future in a thunder of *geta* clops.

Unexpected Gifts

December 25 was an ordinary school day for us, but this year, for the first time, people were talking about Christmas. Something special had arrived, but nobody knew what it could be.

Kato Sensei went down to the City Hall on his bicycle and came back with five big cartons in his cart.

Five big cartons. What could be in them? Where could they come from?

We crowded round, but he pushed us back and called for a squad of volunteers to help him carry the cartons into the classroom. I raised my hand eagerly, too eagerly perhaps, because he passed over me time and time again. Then with the last pick he pointed to me. I was the youngest one he selected and the happiest.

Sensei had us form five teams of four kids each, and together and with great care we hauled the heavy cartons up the stairs to our second-floor classroom.

What could be in those boxes? everybody wondered.

Hey, don't push. I want to see, too.

Finally, we saw Miss Yamada and got to ask her. Where do these come from? What's in them; what's in them?

I don't know, she replied. Let's read what is written on the stamps. Ah, but they are all in English. I can't read it; can you, Kato Sensei? No? And you, Miss Takahashi?

No, the shy music teacher said, but I'm studying it at home.

Now here was a problem. Wise teacher that she was, Miss Yamada was insisting that we learn who the donors were before we could open our packages.

It is only right to ask, she said, so we can acknowledge them, give them our proper thanks. Won't you try to read them, Miss Takahashi?

But young Miss Takahashi was too shy to speak up and expose herself to criticism.

Then a voice rang out from the back of the room. I can read 'em if you want me to.

It was that new girl, Tanabe-san. Now here was another surprise. The crowd made way as she approached the precious packages and inspected the labels with great care.

Ah, she said, relishing the unexpected attention. They all come from America but from different places. I can read 'em to you if you want, but who cares? Let's open 'em now.

Who was this girl to speak so directly?

And when she'd read each label for us, with names like CARE, the Young Men's Christian Association, and the LaLa Foundation, Miss Yamada led us in a proper show of thanks to the people in faraway America, who had thought of us children at Christmastime.

Christmas? We're not Christians.

What does it matter, Tanabe-san said with a shrug, as long as you get some presents?

Presents? That was fine with us. Christmas was okay.

Yamada Sensei opened the first carton, slicing the packing tape with the edge of the tailor's shears. We all gathered round her, eager for a look.

And from the box, she drew out many colorful clothes, American styles for boys and girls. One pair of pants came with red suspenders and everyone laughed at the boy who got them. But that didn't bother Abe-kun. He laughed as loudly as any of them and snapped his red suspenders repeatedly.

Next was a white dress with blue dots and pink ribbons at the waist. It looked fit for a princess, and by chance it fell to Miss Yamada's niece Shizuko, another of the barefoot girls on my *Undo-kai* team. But the boys laughed at the blue-dotted dress, calling it a clown costume. Perhaps, but I would have loved to have had it. Anything with a little color.

This first box was full of beautiful clothes, things I had never seen before. All the boys wanted the blue jeans, so Miss Yamada had to draw lots many times before we knew who got to win them. I wanted some blue jeans too and I deserved them as much as any boy, but Miss Yamada did not see things that way and that was the end of it.

There were ten girls without any indoor shoes at all, half of them *hibakusha*. One of them was Kazuko. It was only fair that Sensei let them pick first. There were still some shoes left after that, however, and she let us other girls draw lots for them. My good luck was with me, for I won my chance, the last pair of the small sizes. They were Buster Browns, the first Western shoes I ever wore, and when I stomped around in them the leather squeaked and they pinched my feet painfully until I finally broke them in. But after that we were inseparable, my Buster Browns and me.

Miss Takahashi presided over the distribution of the second carton. A wonderful smell filled the room as soon as she cut through the wrappings. Inside we found all sorts of strange things: toothpaste and toothbrushes, soaps, and marbles, among them the clear ones with the colors inside. They called them cats' eyes, Abe-kun said, and the boys got so crazy when they saw them that Kato Sensei had to confiscate them.

I had never smelled such fragrances as came from all that soap. Akiko drew close and, gathering the air around her as if to smell it better, went dancing around the room like a butterfly.

Which of you brushed your teeth this morning? asked Yamada Sensei. Please raise your hands.

Hai! Midori-chan was the only one.

Just as I thought, Yamada Sensei said. So she treated us to a discussion about teeth and the importance of keeping them clean, and before we could receive our presents, she made us promise that we would brush them, just the way she showed us.

After lunch we opened the third carton. This was full of packaged food: the long dried noodles the *gaijin* called spaghetti, white sugar, granulated salt, dried beans, and powdered milk. This food Kato Sensei distributed very methodically, making sure we packed our rations carefully in our new backpacks.

The fourth carton was the smallest one. In it was a variety of medical items, such as iodine and aspirin and bandages and medical scissors. The sight of all these supplies brought me back to the time when we'd ripped up sheets and clothing to make dressings, my aunt and me. And I thought of all the sheets and all the linens that we had used to stop up all the blood, and still we didn't have enough.

Why are they sending us this now, Sensei?

It was Octopus Bonze again. He must have read my mind. Frail and weak though he was, he was still coming to class.

Why are they sending us bandages now? he was asking. Is there going to be another war?

Kato Sensei saw no humor in his jesting and took the medicines and locked them in the teachers' storeroom.

The fifth carton was the biggest. It was shaped more like a trapezoid than a rectangle and had taken the most curious path to reach us, but we could not know that then.

The last one, Yamada Sensei said. Let us thank our new friends properly.

We did, and then we watched in silence as she sliced into the heavy cardboard flaps with her shears.

Inside were several smaller boxes. We pressed closely around as Sensei removed the first one and gave it to her niece to open. It was wrapped in thick brown paper, and when she pulled it off, the smell of clean white paper filled our nostrils, bundles and bundles of it. I had never known that paper could have a fragrance, not like that, so deep and rich and full of wondrous possibility.

There were crayons, too, in green boxes, sets and sets of them. Twenty-four colors, her niece counted out. No one had ever seen colors like those on a crayon. Even Midori was amazed. And there were pencils, too, pencils with pink erasers. They too had that interesting fresh smell, but Kato Sensei looked at them and frowned.

Erasers are no good, he said firmly. They encourage laziness. Think before you use your pencil. Then there is no need for an eraser.

Miss Yamada looked at him and smiled carefully. She was the senior teacher at the school but younger than he by a couple of years. She, who taught the younger children, could see plenty of use for erasers. I wanted one badly, of course, but in the end they were given to the hibakusha kids, while we got the crayons and the watercolors.

What else could be in the box? Midori wished for delicious cookies, I for warm gloves. Kazuko wanted blankets now that she had her own shoes.

Only Akiko withdrew from the rest of us. She had taken nothing so far and seemed to lack interest in Christmas. In fact, she was watching Octopus Bonze shivering quietly in the far corner of the classroom.

The Americans

These are from Minnesota, Tanabe said cheerfully, some place called the Lincoln Webster School.

Kato Sensei pulled out a set of drawings: big wooden houses, some tall trees and pretty birds, and letters from a boy and a girl about my age.

Miss Takahashi, shy until this moment, now came forward to look at the letters and explain their possible meaning. After a while she looked up at us and said in English: All children are wishing us to be pleasing and enjoyment their gifts sending from their state of Minnesota.

There were more surprises. One sent the boys into raptures. It was a long box printed with a pair of baseball ball bats crossed like an X. As soon as they saw it, they started to howl. Inside was a baseball and then another one, eight fielders' gloves, and even a catcher's mitt. There were hats, three bats, and a bright-white, five-sided rubber plate.

Sugoi; sugoi; this is great, they said. Even the most sullen of them liked this. Christmas was okay. America was okay.

But they didn't really trust their emotions, these troubled boys. Why should we take anything from America? one of them asked. It was Hiroshi, the biggest troublemaker besides Octopus Bonze.

I remember what it was like before all this, he spat out in adolescent wrath. We had our families; we had our homes. We had pencils. We had clothes, shoes, all the rice we could eat. Our school even had a roof on it that didn't leak. And windows.

Enough. Kato Sensei silenced the boy with a single slap to his head. The sound and speed of the blow shocked us all. Not a word, not a sound, was uttered in the class. Perhaps Sensei too was surprised, for after a moment he collected himself and turned to the boy, Hiroshi.

Well, what about *these* Americans? he asked.

But Hiroshi was too mortified to talk. Sensei turned to us and said, this time in a very low voice so that we all had to listen with care: Perhaps it is time we talked about them.

A good teacher knows when to open the veins of a class, and now was such a moment. And so we talked about this America. Miss Takahashi even spoke again. Her sister had been to Los Angeles. But it was Mr. Kato who led the class. Even Yamada Sensei deferred to him.

It was Akiko who finally said: So, Sensei, they bombed us and killed our parents and families and now they send us Christmas presents?

Aren't you glad to have them? he asked. Because there are still more presents in the box.

Akiko paused and considered her predicament. No and yes, she said.

How so? Kato Sensei asked.

I am happy for everyone, that they got these gifts. They are good things. But who bombed us? Wasn't it America?

Mr. Kato paused to let Akiko's comments settle in the air.

This is the essence of the problem, he began uncomfortably. Our Japan was defeated. Our glorious Japanese forces. You all heard the Emperor's voice.

Many of my comrades, many of your family members, many of the people we loved and took comfort from were lost in those years. Many countries lost people. Our suffering, our sacrifice—

That's over now, Yamada Sensei interjected, speaking now for the first time.

Hai, Kato Sensei said and bowed, for she was his senior at the school.

She acknowledged his bow. Please continue, Kato Sensei.

He bowed again. I was saying, he went on with some difficulty, we must take stock of our situation, reflect upon our fate.

We have two new students with us, she said gently, Tanabe-san and Abe-kun. Perhaps they could tell us what they learned in America.

Here was another surprise. The two made their way from the outermost, frigid edges of our little solar system toward the stove. Both were well dressed, their clothes colorful and well made.

Tanabe-san was the older one and she spoke first. My parents were born in Hawaii, she said, and I was born in the state of Washington. I lived there until I was five or six. Everything was fine there at first, the people were nice, everyone was friendly. But then when the war started . . .

What happened; what happened? we all wanted to know.

They rounded us up and sent us to someplace out in the Utah desert. An internment camp, they called it.

Did you see Indians? somebody asked.

I saw a few, I think. One of our guards was an Indian.

Did he have a bow and arrows? Weren't you worried that they'd scalp you?

No and no, Tanabe-san said. They sent me to school. But it was awfully cold there in the winter. We all had to wear blankets in class.

I lived in an internment camp, too, Abe-kun said, almost proudly. It was in the mountains in Idaho and even colder than in Utah.

Ooooh, we said. They have mountains in America? Higher than Mount Fuji?

Oh, yes, he said. Much higher.

America must be a big country, then.

Yes, he answered. Much bigger than Japan,

Ah. And how did they treat you, Abe-kun?

Okay, I guess, he said with a shrug. I know all about World War II.

Do you? Mr. Kato asked. Perhaps you can tell us what you know.

I know the Atomic Bomb was invented by Albert Einstein. He was a great scientist and he was Jewish and he hated war.

Then why did they drop it? It was Octopus Bonze again, rising from his corner and slowly clopping up to claim some space beside the stove. He was shivering badly. Miss Yamada took a sweater from the first carton and put it on him.

You still haven't answered, Octopus Bonze stated. Why did they drop that bomb?

Perhaps they wanted to win the war, Abe-kun replied softly.

By killing us all?

But that is over now, Nagata-kun, Yamada *Sensei* said gently. The war is over. They have offered us their friendship. What should we do? Should we refuse it?

Now it was Nagata's turn to shrug.

Perhaps we'd better refuse all these Christmas gifts then, send them back, she said softly.

No, no! we children cried. We want to keep them.

But the older ones were not sure what to think. Akiko finally accepted a sweater for her cousin but none for herself. Octopus Bonze kept the one he was wearing but refused anything else, asking, What would be the purpose?

Hiroshi took one of the baseballs and a bat and held it in his hand. Look, he said proudly, pointing to a signature carved in the bat: *Joe DiMaggio.*

Who's that? everyone wanted to know.

You don't know? Abe-kun asked. The great New York Yankee Clipper.

But now all the boys were crowding around Hiroshi, pushing and shoving to get at the balls and gloves, and when Kato Sensei finally dismissed the class, they all raced outside excitedly and began throwing the balls around.

Paper Cranes

Kazuko did not return in the new year. She was gone and that was all there was to it. We tried to visit her, but soon she was lost in a maze of orphanages and transfer centers.

I got to know Tanabe-san after that. Things had not been very easy for her, either. Her father had gone back to Hawaii when the war was over and they were processed out of the camps, but her mother insisted on returning to Japan. They argued and argued over what to do, but they just could not agree. Finally they drew lots, and Tanabe-san came with her mother and her cousin, Abe-kun, first to Osaka and now here to Hiroshima, once their barracks home was built.

Surprisingly to me, both she and Abe-kun really liked America, but to them this was natural. Yes, they had been forced into those internment camps. Tanabe-san did not want to be rude, but it was better than the way we lived.

Abe-kun was even prouder. He had an American passport, and he could read and write and do his numbers in American English.

But their Japanese was not good, and this put them at a disadvantage at first. Yet as their Japanese improved, so did their preference for all things American. You could see it in the way they dressed and what they talked about. So we always called them the Americans.

People talk of a paperless society. I lived in one for years. Until that Christmas, clean, blank paper had been too precious for us to use except on the rarest of occasions.

Mottai-nai, Yamada Sensei insisted. Never waste a sheet. And so we practiced our writing on the back of everything: wrapping paper, envelopes, public notices. We practiced calligraphy wherever we could find space in the margins, and then she coated the scraps of our learning with a paste she knew how to make, and we made *origami.*

American or not, Tanabe-san was the best one in our class at making paper cranes. One day she strung 100 of them on a line and hung them above the windows where our *teru-teru-bozu* used to fly.

What was more interesting was that each crane told a different story. For she had made one for every student, using scraps of our schoolwork.

When we discovered that you could actually *read* these paper cranes by looking at them closely, everybody wanted to see, and there was another mad scamper after lunch to identify our classmates by their writing and calligraphy. Not all the judgments were kind. Soon enough, things got a little out of hand, and one of the boys spazzed out and snapped the string that held the cranes.

When class resumed, Yamada Sensei asked the boy to please go and attach it again, and then she called Tanabe-san forward and asked her to explain to the class what the paper cranes meant. This put Tanabe-san somewhat on the spot with her weak Japanese, but she was never one to lack confidence.

Well, she said rather grandly, what they mean is as simple as the crane itself. No more war. What we need is peace.

New Windows

Two and a half years had slipped down the swift-fingered Motoyasu. Like driftwood on the water, we cannot control the currents, only hope to avoid the rocks as they sweep all downstream.

For two and a half years there had been no windows at school. Many children did not come to class in cold or inclement weather. That was fine with me. It made more space near the stove. I moved up closer to Jupiter, where I belonged.

In the meantime, Kato Sensei had used the thick cardboard of our Christmas cartons to cover the windows. This cut down a lot on the light, but it did keep the worst of the wind out and warmed the place a bit. After a while, some of the boys poked holes in the cardboard with their pencils, and then everybody wanted to peep out at the world.

The truth is, my aunt told me as we walked over the bridge on the first day of school,* they had the glass ready for those windows last November. But it was stolen again. Can you believe it?

That was a long conversation for her. What she hadn't said was that it had been the parents, or those acting as parents, who had worked and scrimped and paid for the new window glass themselves.

So it was with a certain interest that she walked into Honkawa School. There were many adults who'd had the same interest in the window glass as she, and they greeted each other with an understanding nod or bow.

Miss Yamada was there at the door—yes, there was a door now—and she welcomed us with a smile. In her arms was a bouquet of gladiolas, a gift from Midori's parents. I was fascinated by these beautiful flowers. I'd never seen such colors. But my aunt felt uncomfortable making small talk and edged away.

But what was this? There was Mr. Kato, standing next to an empty cardboard carton larger than himself and smiling at us. Inside the classroom, new windows sparkled in their frames. Yes. He'd installed them during the holidays, with help from Miss Yamada's brothers.

Windows! The novelty changed the dynamics of our solar system. No longer were we in tight orbit around our coal stove, where the smallest in mass were thrust farthest from the sun. All that changed, and all the spaces by the new windows were taken within a minute.

Oh, Sensei, I'm hot! Akiko exclaimed, with that mixture of mischief and respect that she infused her voice with when she spoke to him. Oh, Sensei, can I open the window, just for a minute?

Mr. Kato nodded, and when she had opened it and admired the workmanship and shown everyone just how smoothly it opened and closed, a yellow butterfly fluttered into the room. Instinctively, several hands reached to catch it.

Leave the butterfly alone, Miss Yamada called out in her firmest voice. Let this beautiful creature go; let it live. Let it live. It's the first one I've seen in two and a half years. Raise the window up, Akiko-san, and the rest of you, very gently now, sit and let it go. That's right. Slowly, slowly now, let it out the window.

Expressions of Hope and Gratitude

Today is a special day. For two weeks, we have been practicing again and again on waste paper, and finally today we will draw our pictures on the thick white paper we've been saving from that last carton of Christmas.

Our task is to take the clean white surface of the paper and transform it into pictures using the crayons and pastel chalks we got from America. We need to thank the kind people from America. We need to show our gratitude. These are Yamada Sensei's instructions.

Carefully, carefully, I fill the paper with my story, for I know what I am going to draw this time, and my heart and imagination are full of it. What makes it even better is that for this day, at least, I have a whole box of crayons and twenty-four colors to share with my friends.

Midori could not decide what to draw. There were the mountains, or was it better to paint cherry trees by the riverside, just when their buds show their first pink tips?

What do you think, Sensei? Do you think we'll ever see our cherry trees in blossom?

I think we will, Miss Yamada said, but I don't know when, Midori-chan. They're growing; they have healthy shoots. Why not draw them?

But I want to use my favorite color, pink, Midori said sadly. How can I, when they've never bloomed?

Oh, but you can, Midori-chan, the shy Miss Takahashi interjected. Use your pink; use all your colors.

But how? Midori asked. They're too young to blossom.

Draw what you hope to see, she said. Draw what you hope to see and you will draw from your heart.

So we drew what we saw and what we hoped to see: our games, our friends, the foods we longed to eat, the homes we would never see again, cherry blossoms by the river, the marvelous new bridge over the Motoyasu, mountains and flowers, cars and buses, dolls with pretty-colored clothes—all this and more we drew, from our eyes and from our hearts.

One by one we placed our drawings on Mr. Kato's desk for his inspection.

Isn't anyone going to draw the Dome?* he asked.

No one raised a hand.

Wouldn't it be impolite to show that to our new friends? Miss Yamada wondered.

Mr. Kato disagreed. They will see what we see, he said sharply. Then, having made his point, he softened and turned again to the class.

Isn't there anyone who wants to do it? How about you, Hiroshi? he asked. You are good at drawing.

No, Sensei, please, Hiroshi stammered, for no one refused Mr. Kato by choice, except, perhaps, Miss Yamada, and she chose her moments very carefully. I am sorry, Sensei. It's too hard, Hiroshi pleaded.

If Octopus Bonze were still here, he would do it. We all missed that boy, but what could be done?

But death was one thing Kato Sensei understood. It was life that was difficult.

That is the most important building in Hiroshima Prefecture, perhaps in all of our Japan, he said in a voice so low that we strained to hear it.

What? I thought. That ruined thing?

But Sensei, there are ghosts there at night, one girl said. My sister saw them.

I feel afraid every time I see it, Akiko put in. Why don't they tear it down?

The Atomic Bomb Dome, now part of the Hiroshima Peace Memorial Museum. (Courtesy of Dr. Gert L. Laqueur, ABCC)

Mr. Kato smiled slightly. There is talk about making it into a Peace Park, he said, dropping that stern military voice now that he had the class's attention. That was the time we liked him best.

Who, Sensei? What kind of park?

Now Miss Yamada spoke up. Perhaps someone would draw this Peace Park for us, she said. Who will do it? Isn't there anyone who dares?

I will. It was Abe-kun, and he stood up on his orange-crate chair to make sure that everyone saw him.

That set the class astir again, for Abe-kun was different. He wore blue jeans from America. I looked around to see what the others were thinking. No one let on.

But none of that mattered to Abe-kun. I'll draw it just the way it is, he said proudly. That way they'll know I made it here to Hiroshima.

He was what we call a *ni sei*, a Japanese who had been born in America. In Abe's case it was Portland, Oregon, where his father, who was an eighth-generation Buddhist priest from Kyoto, had been sent to set up a temple. Later, after we got to know him, my aunt and I used to go listen to his father chant sutras, for he was a master of the old Kyoto style and dialect that she liked so much.

The following morning on the way to school, I came across Abe-kun in front of the ruined Dome. It was all that remained of a building whose shape or purpose I could no longer recall. He had his sketchpad and a set of colored pencils. Along the riverbanks, new life was pushing through the earth: the cherry trees we had planted with Miss Yamada. And for the first time in two and a half years, there were herons fishing in the water.

How is it, I ask him, that you dare to draw the A Dome? I could never do it.

I don't think it's scary, he said with his customary bravado. I wasn't here when the A-Bomb fell, so I didn't see what happened. So when I look at that dome, all I see is another broken building. What do I care if it makes them happy?

And he laughed that impish, boyish laugh of his and set about his drawing.

Abe-kun had been in a prison camp, so like everyone, I was curious about one thing.

Don't you hate the Americans? I finally asked.

Abe screwed up his nose and thought about that. Hate them? he repeated. No, I don't. A good Buddhist does not hate.

It was really lucky that you weren't killed, I ventured.

I never thought I'd get killed, he responded. It wasn't like that.

So I asked him to tell me what it was like.

Mostly, it was boring, he explained. They'd put a fence around everybody. That was no fun, to be penned up like sheep. And there wasn't much to do, except go to school every day. It was crowded, but his family had a hut of their own and enough to eat. What bothered him the most, he said, was the way some guards looked down on them for being Japanese.

It wasn't fair, he declared. They took away our house and all our furniture. My mother lost a lot of family treasures. But I made a lot of American friends, too, and some of them were very kind. They even helped us get to Japan when we got out of the camp and were trying to figure out where to go.

When we came here, he continued, all we had was one suitcase, my cousin and me. But that was okay, too. The worst was that I had to leave my model airplane behind. There was just no room to take it.

What a strange boy, I thought, that the loss of a model airplane would bother him more than three years in a concentration camp.

A Baton of Cosmos Flowers

At last, our pictures for the kind Americans were completed. Yamada Sensei chose the fifty she liked best and showed them to Principal Sensei. Abe-kun's drawing was so well done that we were certain they'd include it. But no one knew which others had been selected.

Of course, I hoped that mine would be chosen. It had taken me a long time to settle on a topic, and I'd worked very hard on it. It was Akiko who'd suggested the subject. Why not draw the barefoot girls, she said saucily, beating those boys on *Undo-kai?*

And so I closed my eyes and swam against time's flow and summoned from some months past the happy faces, the voices raised expectantly, the baton of cosmos flowers, and there I drew myself, about to cross the finish line. And then among the crowd of spectators, I placed four figures who could never be there, for I had listened to Miss Takahashi and drawn what I'd wanted more than anything else to see: my dear mother, and my sister, brother, and grandmother.

2007

Like most stories, this one has many tellers and many ways to tell it. But Hiroshima is not like other cities: history cleaves to it and to us, its children. Yet history never stands its ground for long. It shifts and sways and cares not if we follow.

The long years passed. We grew around our memories and forgot, or remembered them if we could. I took my medicine when the radiation caught up with me and never lost my hair. I'd had a good life in Hiroshima: an honest husband, two careful daughters, and three big, healthy grandsons. I could have been content with that.

But then one day, I saw my drawing in the *Yomiuri Shimbun* newspaper, and that started me on a road I'd never thought I'd walk. Although I was always curious about America, I had no particular love for it, no wish to know her people or see her cities. But hardly had I put the paper down when the phone started ringing. It was Midori-san, calling from Tokyo.

Oh, Hanako, she squealed with delight, could it be true?

Yes, I told her, they've found our pictures. Did you see it? That's the one I drew!

Oh, I knew it, I knew it, she responded with a laugh.

And soon we were talking and laughing like schoolgirls again and she was making plans for us to visit Washington, D.C.

But I was very wary, and it took her a long time to convince me. I'd made my peace with life and had no need to disturb things

Many people were so badly burnt by the bomb that they looked like yurai *ghosts.* (Drawing by Tomoko Konishi, courtesy of Toshimi Ishida)

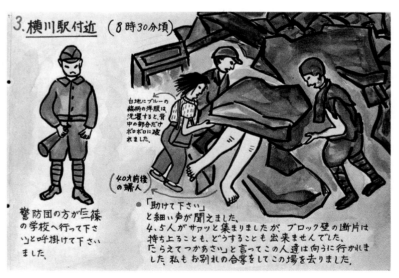

Hiroshima policeman amid the ruins. (Drawing by Tomoko Konishi, courtesy of Toshimi Ishida)

Undo-kai, *Field Day, drawn by Hanako.* (From the collection of All Souls Church, Unitarian, Washington, D.C.)

Nurse tending to the injured in Hiroshima. (Drawing by Tomoko Konishi, courtesy of Toshimi Ishida)

For a month following the bomb, the air stayed black and highly toxic. A typhoon struck in September 1945 and cleared the air, washing tens of thousands out of the river and into the sea. (From the collection of All Souls Church, Unitarian, Washington, D.C.)

Two girls. (Drawing by Tomoko Konishi, courtesy of Toshimi Ishida)

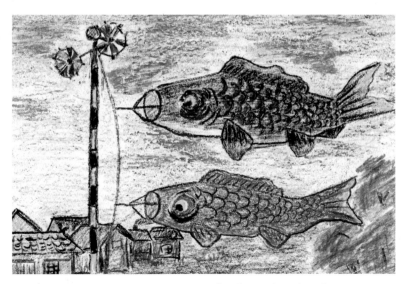

Wind carp. (From the collection of All Souls Church, Unitarian, Washington, D.C.)

Kato Sensei. (From the collection of All Souls Church, Unitarian, Washington, D.C.)

Mrs. Tomoko Furusawa, with the drawing she sent to the U.S. as a child, depicting the Japanese game called tama-wari. (Courtesy of Tomoko Furusawa)

Cherry blossoms along the Motoyasu River. (From the collection of All Souls Church, Unitarian, Washington, D.C.)

The Dome. (From the collection of All Souls Church, Unitarian, Washington, D.C.)

Toshimi Ishida with his drawing. (Courtesy of Toshimi Ishida)

further. In the end, though, her enthusiasm won me over, and once we were there and had visited the famous cherry trees, walked the streets, and seen the White House and the Smithsonian museums, I began to feel more confident.

The real purpose of our trip, of course, was to visit the All Souls Church. For it was to these kind people that our pictures had been sent nearly sixty years before, and we were very curious to see them and know just how it happened.

Our hosts received us with great politeness, as if we might be made of china. Little did they know what tough old birds we were. Still, I was as nervous and twittering as a sparrow when they brought out the cardboard box that held our pictures and laid it on the table. But Midori-san was calm. Thank goodness I had her with me.

I watched with trepidation as they pulled the packet out, forty-eight pictures wrapped in plain white paper. They were a bit brittle and slightly yellowed but still marvelously alive with color and the rich vitality of youth.

Look! Midori exclaimed and pointed excitedly. There's your drawing of *Undo-kai*. And sure enough, it was lying on the top of the pile.

Oh, it's beautiful, she said, and she chatted gaily with our translator about what it meant, but it was all I could do to keep from crying.

Then when I'd had some tea and we began to study the other drawings one by one, I could not help but join in Midori's joy and laughter. What a flood of emotions those old pictures unleashed as we pointed to the once-familiar sights, remembering our classmates and trying to recall who drew each one and why.

It was our hosts who showed us the article from *Time* magazine. That told it better than I ever could. It was dated November 1946, and there, under a headline reading *ATOMIC AGE Angel Food*, was a photograph that took our breath away—two admirals and a beaming wife, cutting a cake baked in the shape of a mushroom cloud.

Midori, who just moments before had been taking such delight in our drawings, suggesting that we bring them back to Hiroshima for an exhibition, nearly fainted when she saw it and refused to look at the article any further.

But I was curious. We'd come this far. I asked one of our hosts if she could translate.

Well, she explained, it seems that they'd baked this thing to celebrate the completion of some nuclear tests on Bikini Island.

Great, I heard Midori say. As if Hiroshima and Nagasaki were not enough.

Well, not everyone was happy about it, our host assured us. That's where our church came in. Our minister, Rev. A. Powell Davies, was as angry as Moses. That's what *Time* says.

As angry as Moses—I had to smile a little at that. She saw that and read on.

How would it seem in Hiroshima or Nagasaki to know that Americans make cakes of angel-food puffs in the image of that terrible diabolical thing? Dr. Davies had thundered from the pulpit of the All Souls Church. If I had the authority of a priest of the Middle Ages, he said, I would call down the wrath of God upon such an obscenity, such a monstrous betrayal of everything for which the broken-hearted of the world are waiting.

These were probably the harshest words ever spoken about a dessert. Yes, our host remarked with a smile. That's what *Time* said.

What a country, where even a cake can have a story. This one owed its creation to some bakers in East St. Louis who had sent it to Washington for the celebration. According to a bakery salesman who helped design it, they had intended it as nothing more than something good to eat.

But the Lord works in mysterious ways, as our church hosts might have said. Dr. Davies' denunciation made its way quickly to Tokyo, for *Time* had a long reach then, and when it came to the attention of General MacArthur, which was very shortly indeed, he was not pleased by the distraction.

Ah, said Midori warmly, now that she had recovered from her shock. That's where Dr. Bell comes in. He worked for MacArthur. I remember the day he came to our school. Don't you, Hanako? It was so cold that day my cheeks froze red.

Rev. A. Powell Davies condemning the mushroom-cloud cake. (From the collection of All Souls Church, Unitarian, Washington, D.C.)

Oh, I remembered. Which day wasn't cold? Everyone remembered Dr. Bell at Honkawa School.

Yes, our host was saying, he was the one who wrote to Dr. Davies, suggesting that perhaps our church could show the Japanese people another, better, side of America. That's what we did, I guess, she added with a smile. And so indeed they had.

We left our new friends at the church with pictures of our pictures and warm memories, marveling at the ways of the world and how a cake could set a chain of events in motion that would lead from a church in Washington, D.C. to MacArthur's office in Tokyo, and then to the visit of Dr. Bell, our unexpected Christmas gifts, and eventually our expressions of hope and gratitude.

Our drawings had a few months of unexpected fame, for the U.S. State Department borrowed them from the church and sent

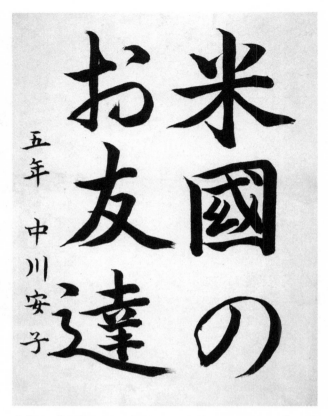

Calligraphy depicting the message: America is our friend.
(From the collection of All Souls Church, Unitarian,
Washington, D.C.)

them on a traveling exhibit. But soon enough they were put aside
as the children's work they were.

As for me, it's strange, but once I had seen my drawing again,
been to America, and held a piece of my past between my aging
fingers, a door to the room I'd built to hide my memory in
appeared. And all I had to do was walk through it to see my
mother again, standing there with her pink parasol, shading
Grandmother from the sun, and watching me run.

Appendix

U.S.-Japan Chronology, 1854-1956

1854—Commodore Matthew Perry signs a trade treaty with the Japanese shogun, signaling the beginning of U.S.-Japanese relations.

1860—A Japanese embassy is established in Washington, D.C.

1868—The Meiji Restoration begins, and Emperor Meiji assumes power.

1898—The U.S. annexes Hawaii; U.S. seizes the Philippines from Spain in the Spanish-American War.

1906—Pres. Theodore Roosevelt wins the Nobel Prize for ending the Russo-Japanese war.

1907—The "Gentlemen's Agreement" limits Japanese immigration to the U.S.

1912—Three thousand cherry trees, a gift from the city of Tokyo, are planted along the Potomac River in Washington, D.C.

1931—Japan occupies Manchuria in northern China.

1937—Japanese forces overrun Nanking, China.

1940—Germany, Italy, and Japan sign the Tri-Partite Pact.

1941—U.S.-Japanese talks fail; the Japanese attack Pearl Harbor.

1942—The U.S. begins interning Japanese-Americans in special camps; the Japanese empire reaches its fullest extent with the conquest of Indochina, the Philippines, Siam, Burma, Malaysia, Singapore, and Indonesia.

1945—Hiroshima and Nagasaki are bombed; Japan surrenders; and U.S. military occupation of Japan begins under General MacArthur.

1947—A new Japanese constitution expands democracy and limits the military.

1952—Formal U.S. military occupation of Japan ends, and the U.S. and Japan sign the Treaty of Mutual Cooperation and Security.

1955—The Hiroshima Peace Park is dedicated.

1956—Japan joins the United Nations.

Glossary

ABCC. The Atomic Bomb Casualty Commission, opened by the U.S. in 1946.

ainoko. A child with one Japanese and one foreign parent.

Atomic Bomb Dome. The old Hiroshima Prefectural Hall, a shell of which remained standing after the Atomic Bomb. It became a central part of the Hiroshima Peace Park, which was recognized as a UNESCO World Heritage Site in 1996.

beigun. U.S. military forces.

dogeza. An apology begging for forgiveness, whereby an individual goes down on his knees and touches his forehead to the ground.

Edo time. Period beginning in 1603 with the Tokugawa shogun (ruler of Japan) and ending with the emperor's return to power under the Meiji Restoration of 1868. During most of this time, Nagasaki was the only port open to foreigners.

first day of school. In Japan, the school year begins in early April.

gaijin. Foreigners.

gassho. Joining one's hands together next to the heart, as a sign of respect or prayer.

geta. A sandal or clog, usually of wood, built on platforms, to raise the feet above the ground or mud.

Hamai, Deputy Mayor Shinzo. Hiroshima's first directly elected mayor. Sometimes called the father of Hiroshima, he was a prime force in the city's postwar revitalization and the creation of the Hiroshima Peace Park.

Mushroom cloud. (Drawing by Yoshiko Jaeggi, courtesy of Shizumi Shigeto Manale)

Hiroshima. U.S. military planners deliberately spared the city from bombing during the last months of the war in order to observe the effects of the Atomic Bomb in pristine conditions.

Hiroshima Prefectural Hall. Built in 1915 and originally called the Hiroshima Prefectural Commercial Exhibition. Later it became a central part of the Hiroshima Peace Park.

juban. A garment worn under a kimono.

kibi-dango. Steamed sweet dumplings made of rice powder and sugar.

Little Boy. One of two designs for the Atomic Bombs dropped on Hiroshima and Nagasaki. The other was called Fat Boy.

Lord Ebisu. One of the seven lucky gods, particularly associated with fishing and harvesting.

meisen monpe. Baggy work pants made of low-quality silk, usually for women.

Miyazawa, Kenji. Famous Japanese poet.

ni sei. A child born overseas of a Japanese parent.

okonomiyaki. Pancakes made with chopped Japanese cabbage, meat, eggs, seaweed stock, and wheat flour and cooked in an iron skillet.

omamori. A good-luck charm consisting of one or two silver bells, usually from a Buddhist temple or Shinto shrine.

seiza. A posture of respect, sitting on bent knees with back straight.

tama-wari. A children's game where two teams attempt to toss white and red balls or beanbags into a basket at the top of a long pole. Whichever team puts the most balls or beanbags in the basket wins.

wara-zori. Ancient style of Japanese sandals, made of straw.

yubi-kiri-genman. "Pinky swearing."

yurai. Ghosts that wander restlessly on earth until the cause of their death can be rectified or they receive a proper burial.

Suggested Reading

Acheson, Dean. *Present at the Creation: My Years at the State Department.* New York: W. W. Norton, 1969.

Alperovitz, Gar. *Atomic Diplomacy: Hiroshima and Potsdam—the Use of the Atomic Bomb and the American Confrontation with Soviet Power.* New York: Simon & Schuster, 1965.

Hachiya, Michihiko. *Hiroshima Diary: The Journal of a Japanese Physician, August 6-September 30, 1945.* Translated and edited by Warner Wells. Chapel Hill: University of North Carolina Press, 1955.

Hall, John Whitney. *Japan from Prehistory to Modern Times.* New York: Dell, 1970.

Hasewaga, Tsuyoshi. *Racing with the Enemy: Stalin, Truman and the Surrender of Japan.* Cambridge, MA: Harvard University Press, 2005.

Hersey, John. *Hiroshima.* New York: Alfred A. Knopf, 1946.

McCullough, David. *Truman.* New York: Simon & Schuster, 1992.

Manchester, William. *American Caesar: Douglas MacArthur 1880-1964.* New York: Little, Brown, 1978.

Spector, Ronald H. *In the Ruins of Empire: the Japanese Surrender and the Battle for Postwar Asia.* New York: Random House, 2007.

Toland, John. *The Rising Sun: The Decline and Fall of the Japanese Empire, 1936-1945.* New York: Random House, 1970.

Yep, Laurence. *Hiroshima.* New York: Scholastic, 1995.

For Youth

Coerr, Eleanor. *Sadako and the Thousand Paper Cranes.* New York, Putnam's Sons, 1977.

Authors' Note

Running with Cosmos Flowers is in many ways the culmination of my life's work. The main character of the book, Hanako, is a soul into whom I have compressed all the information, events, and experiences I have gathered over many years. I was born in Hiroshima after the war. My mother and many of her family were teachers in schools near the city and personally witnessed the destruction resulting from the Atomic Bomb. In 1985, the Bay Area Peace Committee asked me to create a dance and poetry performance for the fortieth anniversary of the Hiroshima and Nagasaki bombings. In preparation, I revisited Hiroshima, interviewed many survivors, and had many conversations with my mother and other relatives about their experiences. Since then, I have made numerous return visits to the city and interviewed dozens of people who directly experienced the events of August 1945. In 2006, while accompanying four Hiroshima and Nagasaki survivors to the All Souls Church, Unitarian, in Washington, D.C., I first came across the forty-eight drawings that the children from Honkawa School had sent in 1948. When I saw how bright and hopeful they were, so unlike the dark, tortured drawings I expected, it seemed like a miracle to me. As a mother and artist, I was inspired by their painful yet cheerful expressions to tell their story. It's my hope that they will inspire others, too.

Shizumi Shigeto Manale

It has been my privilege to work with Shizumi-san on this book in one form or another for several years and help her bring the story of Hanako and the children of the Honkawa School to readers in the United States for the first time. Few events over the past century have been as controversial as the bombing of Hiroshima, and there are many lenses through which to view its causes and its consequences. We hope that *Running with Cosmos Flowers* will add another voice to that discussion, that of the children who survived.

Richard Marshall

Acknowledgments

We wish to thank many people for their help. First and foremost are the bomb survivors Kiyoko Imori, Keiji Nakazawa, Tamiko Nishimoto, Shotaro Kodama, Kazuhiro Yoshimura, and Yoshio Sato. Their courage and positive nature have been an inspiration to us from the very beginning. Our particular thanks go to Hiroshima's Honkawa Elementary School: Principal Kazunori Kono; teachers Susumu Kaya and Setsuko Yamagiwa; and Alumni Association members Toshimi Ishida, Misako Shimomura, Koki Abiko, Tomoko Iwamoto, Genji Higashikawa, Yoshiko Ito, Hiroko Nakajima, Yoshihiro Nishimura, Yoshie Fujii, Setsuko Noma, Akihisa Yagi, Rumi Tanaka, Junko Hotta, Kaeko Taida, Akinobu Harada, Satoshi Aohara, Toshikuni Sera, and volunteer Fumiko Kojima.

The All Souls Church, Unitarian, Washington, D.C. played an integral part in our story. We would like to express our gratitude to Rev. Robert Hardies; Rev. Louise Green; Jane and Paul Pfeiffer; and the members of the Hiroshima Children's Drawing Committee, Charles Wooldridge, Mr. and Mrs. Robert Freeman, Melvin Hardy, Judith Bauer, Barbara Corprew, and Emily Dyer for their cooperation and permission to use some of the wonderful drawings from the Honkawa schoolchildren in our book.

We offer a special thanks to Elissa Leif, Gretchen Jones, Satako Wakita, Kohei Kusita, and Koki Abiko, who helped translate Shizumi's original Japanese text into English, and to our agent, Anne Devlin, whose encouragement and diligence led us to

Pelican Publishing and our editor, Nina Kooij. We would like to thank Midori Nosohara, Hiroshi Fujimura, Michiyo Goto, Kaori Ooishi, Ayako Sato, Shoji Sato, Kazunari Ikeda, Yoshiharu Kawara, Soroputimist Itsukushima Hiroshima, David Pitts, Yoshi Manale, and Clare Marshall for reading early versions of our manuscript. Michael Singer, Joan Grant, and Carol Hiergert gave us great help with their patient and careful proofreading. Kazuko Yasutake helped us greatly with photo editing. Zakia Marshall has lent us valuable support, from taming balky computers and formatting files and CDs to building our Web site. Particular thanks go to Andrew Manale for hosting many *hibakusha* at the Manale home in Silver Spring and for his long year of support for Shizumi's Hiroshima projects.

We would like to thank Yoshiko Jaeggi for her illustrations and Tomoko Konishi for permission to use her drawings. The Ninoshima Orphanage Gakuen provided valuable information on conditions in the orphanages at the end of the war. We appreciate the help of Mrs. Mizoguchi and the Fukuroimachi Elementary School, and wish to thank Steve Leeper, formerly of the Hiroshima Peace Foundation, and John Steinbach and Sayuri Miyazaki of the Washington, D.C. Hiroshima Nagasaki Peace Committee for their encouragement and professional advice. And finally, thanks to Katherine Laqueur Larson for permission to use her father's photograph of Hiroshima's Dome.